Fargo either had to wait until they went back to leaning and talking, or do what he did. He was up in a blur and drove the toothpick's double-edged blade into the chest of the man who was stretching. He twisted, yanked it out, and was on the second Tong before the first realized he had been stabbed. The second man turned right into the toothpick. Fargo sank the sharp steel to the hilt in the man's throat and slashed outward.

It had been beautifully done. Neither managed to utter an outcry. They thrashed a bit, and the second man gurgled and bubbled fountains of blood. . . .

The Trailsman

Beginnings . . . they bend the tree and they mark the man. Skye Fargo was born when he was eighteen. Terror was his midwife, vengeance his first cry. Killing spawned Skye Fargo, ruthless, cold-blooded murder. Out of the acrid smoke of gunpowder still hanging in the air, he rose, cried out a promise never forgotten.

The Trailsman they began to call him all across the West: searcher, scout, hunter, the man who could see where others only looked, his skills for hire but not his soul, the man who lived each day to the fullest, yet trailed each tomorrow. Skye Fargo, the Trailsman, the seeker who could take the wildness of a land and the wanting of a woman and make them his own.

The remote and rugged mountains of
Utah Territory, 1861—where a hatchet in the back
was a common way to die.

1

The mountains were green and lush with life, and deadly to man and beast alike.

Skye Fargo caught sight of a careless buck in a thicket. The buck heard the clomp of the Ovaro's hooves and raised its head for a look and ducked down again.

Drawing rein, Fargo sat as still as a statue with his Henry pressed to his shoulder and his cheek to the smooth brass, waiting for the buck to stick its head up again. He hadn't had a good meal in a week. The prospect of a thick venison steak made his mouth water.

The buck wasn't making the same mistake twice.

Fargo tried a trick. He whistled as high and as loud as he could, and the curious buck rose up for another look. "Got you," Fargo said to himself, and stroked the trigger.

"I can taste the meat already," Fargo said as he shoved the Henry into the saddle scabbard. He was talking to himself a lot of late. Alighting, he led the Ovaro to the thicket.

Retrieving the buck took effort. The bushes were so close together that it was a wonder the buck had wormed its way in. But bucks were good at hiding. He once saw a hunter walk right past one lying in tall grass and not notice it.

After a lot of pulling and grunting, Fargo got this one out of the thicket. Drawing his Arkansas toothpick from its ankle sheath, he set to work.

Most men would use a skinning knife or a bowie but he was partial to the toothpick. Double-edged and sharp as a razor, it was light and slender enough that he could whip it out quickly if he had to.

Fargo didn't bother with fancy carving. He had no intention of saving and curing the hide; it was the meat he wanted. He impaled a hunk of haunch on a spit, kindled a fire, and sat watching the meat cook. His stomach rumbled and the aroma about made him want to bite into the meat raw.

It was as he was squatting there, his forearms across his knees, that the undergrowth crackled.

Instantly Fargo was erect with his hand on his Colt. A tall man, broad at the shoulders, he wore buckskins and boots and a white hat and red bandanna. All had seen a lot of use.

Out of the woods came three men. To say Fargo was surprised was putting it mildly. For one thing, he wasn't aware of a town or settlement nearby. For another, the three were Chinese.

One was short and thin and had a weasel face that Fargo took a dislike to on sight. The man wore the usual Chinese garb and a small hat that made Fargo think of an upside-down food bowl. The man stopped and whispered something to his companions.

The other two were squat and thick and wore matching black clothes. They listened and gave slight bobs of their heads. Both stuck their hands up their baggy sleeves and crossed their arms across their chests as they followed the weasel over.

"So sorry, sir," the weasel said, "for disturbing you at your meal."

"What do you want?" Fargo demanded. He had nothing against the Chinese. He didn't hate them as many whites did simply because they weren't white. But strangers too often spelled trouble, Chinese or otherwise.

"I am Lo Ping." The man gestured at the pair in black. "My associates are the Hu brothers."

"Good for you." Fargo was so hungry, his gut hurt. He wanted them to leave so he could get to eating.

Lo Ping smiled but it didn't touch his eyes. "We wonder if you have perhaps seen anyone in the past hour or so. We seek a girl who ran away from Hunan."

"Hunan?" Fargo repeated. "Who or what is that?"

"It is a gold camp, good sir," Lo Ping said. "Named after a province in China from which many of us at the camp are from."

"A gold camp this far out?" Fargo recollected that the last outpost he'd come across was fifty miles back.

Lo Ping nodded. "It is a new one. Run by Chinese, for Chinese."

"That's a first," Fargo said. He'd been to camps where Chinese made up part of the population but never to one exclusively so.

"About the girl," Lo Ping said. "Have you seen her, perhaps?"

"All I've seen is him," Fargo answered, with a nod at the buck. "And you."

"Ah." Lo Ping frowned. "Again, I am sorry to have disturbed you. We will depart." He started to turn but stopped. "If you should see her, and if you would bring her to Hunan, there will be a suitable reward."

"What is she? An outlaw?" Fargo joked.

"As I told you, she is a runaway," Lo Ping said. "She is most temperamental and does not like to do as she is told."

"Who does?" Fargo said.

"She dishonors her ancestors with her behavior," Lo Ping elaborated, with a hint of anger. "She has been paid for, and should accept her fate as everyone else does. We all have our purpose."

"I doubt I'll see her," Fargo said. "As soon as I'm done eating, I'll be on my way."

"That is good, sir," Lo Ping said.

Something in the man's tone rankled, a suggestion that Fargo was unwelcome. He tested his hunch by asking, "Is there a general store in this gold camp of yours? I could stand to buy some supplies."

Lo Ping frowned. "There is, but it does not carry much you can use."

"How the hell would you know?"

"It caters to Chinese needs," Lo Ping said. "Trust me when I say it would be wiser for you to buy your supplies elsewhere." He smiled and bobbed his head and walked off.

3

Moving as one, the Hu brothers turned and trailed after him.

Fargo shook his head in amusement. He didn't really need supplies and didn't give a damn about their gold camp. As soon as he finished eating, he'd move on.

Sinking back down, he breathed deep of the delicious aroma, and practically drooled. He was nothing if not patient, and he waited until the meat was cooked clear through before he removed the spit from the fire. He didn't bother taking it off the stick. Holding an end in either hand, he tore into the juicy venison with relish.

He liked beef more and buffalo best but deer meat was delicious in its own right. Closing his eyes, he chewed with the eagerness of a starved wolf.

When he opened his eyes, a girl was there.

She'd stepped from behind a tall spruce and stood eyeing him uncertainly. To call her a "girl" wasn't quite fitting; she was in her twenties, he reckoned, and her womanly attributes were enough to draw a man's eye despite her loose-fitting clothes. She wasn't wearing a dress. She had on a Chinese-style shirt and pants similar to those the three men had worn, and sandals. Her black hair was cropped at the shoulders. Her eyes were a penetrating brown, her full lips inviting.

Fargo stopped chewing and said with his mouth full, "Well, now."

She gnawed her lower lip and gazed nervously in the direction Lo Ping and the Hu brothers had gone.

"Who might you be?" Fargo asked.

She stared at him.

"Do you speak English?"

All she did was stare.

"Are you hungry?" Fargo said, motioning at the buck. "I have plenty to spare." He waited but when all she did was continue to stare, he shrugged and took another bite.

The girl inched closer. She seemed undecided if she could trust him.

On an impulse Fargo cut off a piece and held it out to her. "Here."

She stopped and did more staring.

4

"You're damn ridiculous," Fargo said, and tossed the piece at her feet.

Warily, almost timidly, she tucked at the knees and carefully plucked the meat from the ground. She sniffed it a few times, then brushed it off and tried a tiny bite. Evidently she wasn't used to eating deer. She swallowed, and smiled, and bit off a bigger mouthful.

"That's more like it," Fargo said. He indicated a spot across the fire. "You're welcome to join me if you'd like."

She understood. She eased down cross-legged and regarded him with what he took to be more than casual interest.

"Skye Fargo," he introduced himself, and tapped his chest. He pointed at her. "What's your name?"

She didn't respond.

"Name," Fargo said. He tapped his chest again. "Fargo." He pointed at her and arched his brows.

She took another bite of venison.

"Oh, well." Fargo shrugged. He hadn't had many dealings with the Chinese, and while he spoke Spanish and could hold up his end of a conversation in half a dozen Indian tongues, he didn't know a lick of her language.

She finished and wiped her fingers on the grass. "May I please have another piece, kind sir? It is very good and I am starved."

Fargo glanced up. "So you do know English?" He took the toothpick from his lap. "You can have as much as you'd like." He cut off a larger chunk and tossed it across the fire.

She deftly snatched it out of the air. "Thank you very much. It has been two days since I ate last."

"You're the one those gents were after," Fargo said. "The girl who ran away from the gold camp."

"Did they tell you why?"

"Something about you don't like being told what to do," Fargo recollected.

"There is more to it than that," she said. "I refuse to let a man touch me if I do not want him to."

Fargo thought he savvied. "Does Lo Ping want to get in those pants of yours?"

5

"Get in my—?" she said, and her cheeks became pink. "Oh. No. It is not like that. I would not have him for my man if he were the last man on earth."

Fargo laughed.

"I refuse to work for Madame Lotus and ran away. Han sent Lo Ping and his hatchet men after me."

"Hatchet men?" Fargo said.

"Yes. They—" She looked past him, and stiffened and pushed to her feet.

Fargo suspected what he would see before he turned.

Lo Ping and the Hu brothers were back. Lo Ping smiled his oily smile and crooked a finger at the girl. "We have found you. You will come along and not cause trouble."

"I will not," the girl declared.

"You have no choice."

Fargo couldn't say what made him do what he did next. Maybe it was how Lo Ping made his skin crawl. Maybe he didn't like to see the girl bullied. Or maybe he was just pissed that they kept interrupting his meal. Whatever his reason, he stood and faced them and said, "Sure she does."

Lo Ping scowled. "This is not your concern. Leave her to us and go about your business."

"And if I don't?" Fargo said.

"You will be taught a lesson in manners," Lo Ping warned. "And it will not be pleasant."

2

Skye Fargo set the spit down and placed his hand on his Colt. "I don't take kindly to being threatened, you little peckerwood."

"I do not know what a peckerwood is. But it was not a threat. It was a warning," Lo Ping said. "You are meddling in matters that do not concern you, and my master will be most displeased."

"Whose boots do you lick?"

"I beg your pardon?"

"You said you have a master."

"Master Han," Lo Ping clarified. "I am in his employ. The Hu brothers, as well." He glared at the girl. "Mai Wing, too, although she refuses to admit it."

Mai Wing clenched her small fists. "I was not given a say in the matter."

"You disobeyed, woman," Lo Ping spat. "You have shamed yourself and those who bore you. And now you seek to shame Master Han."

"It is not shameful to want to live. I want to live and not as he wants me to," Mai Wing said.

Lo Ping motioned at the stoic Hu brothers and said something in Chinese.

The pair started forward but halted when Fargo moved between them and the girl. "This is where you skedaddle, mister. And take the gents in black with you."

"Have a care," Lo Ping said.

"What I have," Fargo said, "is a six-shooter." With a lightning flick of his hand, the Colt was out and leveled at Lo

Ping. "Go back to your master and tell him I said you couldn't have her."

"You know not what you do."

"I won't say it twice," Fargo said.

Lo Ping was a study in barely suppressed fury. "That is the one trait I like least of your kind. Your perpetual arrogance."

"My kind?"

"White people."

"So you're one of those," Fargo said. He wagged the Colt. "Light a shuck while you still can."

Lo Ping drew himself up to his full less than considerable height. "You will regret this."

"The only thing I regret," Fargo said, "is listening to you flap your gums." To stress his point, he cocked the Colt.

The Hu brothers might as well have been chiseled from stone for all the emotion they showed. They were staring at Lo Ping as if awaiting instructions.

Lo Ping bared his teeth in a snarl. "We will go. But not because you have the better of us."

"If that's what you want to tell yourself," Fargo said.

"Clever talk and a domineering way do not have anything to do with being man at his best."

"What in hell are you talking about?"

"I quote Confucius."

"Who?"

Lo Ping smirked. "Arrogance and ignorance often go hand in hand."

"So do being stupid and lead poisoning," Fargo said, and raised the Colt.

"I can see there is no reasoning with you." Lo Ping turned. "You have not heard the last of us." He barked words in Chinese and stalked into the trees. As before, the Hu brothers dutifully followed.

"I thank you for your help," Mai Wing said, "but you have made an enemy."

"I've made them before."

"I am not talking about Lo Ping or the Hus. I am talking about Master Han."

8

"Never met the gent," Fargo said. He was listening to the retreating footfalls of the three Chinese. They were about as quiet in the woods as cows.

"By thwarting Lo Ping, you have thwarted Master Han. He is a most evil man."

Fargo deemed it safe to sink back down and pick up his venison. "Where did you learn English?" he asked by way of small talk.

"From a missionary. Father William. He was very kind. It saddened me that I could not convert to his faith as he wanted me to do."

Fargo had to hand it to her. She spoke better English than he did. He noticed, too, the swell of her breasts under her shirt. It was hard to tell exactly, with her clothes so loose, but he'd bet his poke she had tits the size of melons.

"What are you looking at?" Mai Wing asked.

"Your buttons," Fargo lied, and bit off a chunk of meat. It had grown cold and he growled in annoyance.

"You make strange sounds."

"I do that a lot." Fargo cut off another strip for her and flipped it over the flames.

"You Americans are a mystery to me," Mai Wing said. "You do not think or act like we Chinese."

"I reckon we fuck the same," Fargo said.

Mai Wing froze with the meat halfway to her mouth. "Did you just say 'fuck'?"

"That's what my ears heard." Fargo grinned and winked and chewed.

"I have been told it is a word not to be used in the company of a lady."

"So some say," Fargo said. "But even ladies like a frolic under the sheets."

"You are most remarkable," Mai Wing said, and lapsed into a thoughtful silence.

Fargo chuckled, remembering the time he got into a discussion with a churchgoing gal about the finer points of lovemaking, and how she'd blushed from her toes to her hairline. Yet later that night she had humped his brains out.

"May I ask you a question?"

"Are you always so damn polite?" Fargo rejoined.

"We are taught to be courteous from an early age," Mai Wing said. "It is our nature to always show respect toward others."

"Hell," Fargo said. "I'd make a terrible Chinaman."

"You don't show respect to others?"

"When they earn it."

"Most remarkable," Mai Wing said again.

An awkward silence fell, and to break it, Fargo said, "Tell me how you ended up at this camp. What's it called again?"

"Hunan. Master Han has named it after the province he is from. There were some who wanted to give it a different name but they dared not oppose him."

"How did you get there?" Fargo prompted when she didn't go on.

Mai Wing frowned. "I came to America for the same reason so many of my people do. Opportunity. In China there are a great many people and not so many jobs. Here there is plenty of work. I came with my parents and my grandfather." Her frown deepened. "My father loved your country. He loved everything about it. He looked forward to much prosperity. But he and my mother took ill on the ship and both died before we ever reached your shores."

"Sorry to hear," Fargo said.

"Now I live with my grandfather. And he lives in perpetual fear."

"Of what?"

"Of whom," Mai Wing said. "Of Master Han, who runs the camp with a fist of iron."

"Why do the people put up with it?"

"What can they do?" Mai Wing countered. "In China they were peasants. They led simple lives. They do not know how to fight. They can't stand up to the Tong."

"The who?"

"The what," Mai Wing corrected him again. "They call themselves a benevolent society but they are anything but. Master Han was high in the councils of the Dragon Tong back in China. He has dozens of hatchet men who obey his every whim."

"Men like the Hu brothers?"

Mai Wing nodded. "Master Han has only to snap his fingers and they will bury a hatchet in whomever he wants slain."

"Are there any whites in this gold camp?"

"A few have not left," Mai Wing said. "But they are as cowed as everyone else. The man who runs the general store you asked about is white. And there is a blacksmith. He is big and bold but even he dares not defy Master Han and the Tong."

"Seems to me someone should put this Han in his place," Fargo remarked.

"You know not what you say," Mai Wing said. "It is easy to contemplate but impossible to do."

"Nothing's impossible," Fargo said. He cut more meat for both of them.

Mai Wing grew pensive. She glanced at him several times and finally paused with a piece halfway to her mouth. "I have a request."

"You want me to make love to you?"

"What? No." Mai Wing cocked her head. "Why do you keep bringing up sex?"

"You're female. I'm male."

Mai Wing started to laugh but caught herself. "Father William warned me about men like you. He said sex is all some Americans think of."

"Smart man," Fargo said.

"He was very wise. But my request does not have to do with that."

Fargo sighed. "Figures. What, then?"

"I humbly ask that you take me with you."

Now it was Fargo who paused. "You don't know where I'm headed."

"It does not matter. I can't go back to Hunan. If I do, Master Han will punish me. Or Madame Lotus will, and she is worse when it comes to women. There is no telling what she will do. She is capable of anything."

"What about your grandpa?"

"I told him I was leaving the camp and begged him to come with me but he refused. He is too afraid of Master

11

Han and the Tong." Mai Wing sat up. "Will you take me? I promise not be a bother, as you would say."

"I don't know," Fargo hedged. They'd have to ride double and it would take a week or more to reach the next town. But she did have a nice body, and those unusually large tits for a Chinese gal.

"Please," Mai Wing said. "If you don't, I must make my way through this wilderness on my own."

Fargo snorted. On foot, she stood a snowball's chance in hell of making it out of the mountains. "How far did you aim to go?"

"I was thinking I would return to San Francisco. It is where our ship docked and there are many Chinese."

"I know. I've been there. But San Francisco is to the west and I'm heading east."

"The direction is not important. Only that I am free."

"I reckon I could take you as far as Virginia City," Fargo said, more to himself than to her.

"There are Chinese there, too, I have heard," Mai Wing said. "It would do as well as—" She stopped and her eyes widened.

Fargo heard the rush of footsteps and started to turn. He glimpsed a pair of figures in black and realized it was the Hu brothers a split second before the side of his head exploded in pain and his consciousness was sucked into a great black hole.

3

Fargo came around with a start and a groan. He was on his back, his left leg bent under him and hurting like hell. His head was worse. It pounded to the beat of an invisible hammer. Propping himself up on his elbows, he slowly rose high enough to look around.

The Ovaro was where he had tied it, thank God. He moved his hand to his holster and was relieved to find the Colt was still there. His hat was upside down next to him.

The fire had burned to a few red embers. Flies buzzed about the dead buck.

There was no sign of Mai Wing.

Gritting his teeth against the pain, Fargo sat up. He gingerly explored his head above his ear and found a lump the size of a hen's egg. No blood, though. Evidently, whichever of the Hu brothers struck him did so with the flat of the hatchet and not the edge.

"Bastards," Fargo growled, and carefully placed his hat back on. Getting to his feet, he roved in a circle, probing the woods.

The girl and her captors were long gone.

Bubbling with anger, Fargo went about gathering additional firewood. He rekindled the flames, half filled his coffeepot with water from his canteen, and put coffee on.

Sullen with anger, he sat and brooded. He had a decision to make. He could forget about Mai Wing and continue on east—or he could pay the gold camp a visit.

He didn't owe the girl anything. They were strangers who happened to meet in the middle of nowhere and shared

a few pieces of venison. He was under no obligation to her whatsoever.

Fargo put a hand to the lump, and winced. He wasn't one to turn the other cheek. When someone hit him, he hit back. When they shot at him, he shot back. The Hu brothers, at Lo Ping's instigation, had given him a hen's egg.

He'd like to repay the favor.

Presently the coffee was ready and he sipped the first cup. Should he leave it be? A smart gent would. A smart gent would get on his horse and light a shuck for anywhere but the gold camp.

He thought about Mai Wing. How she was being forced to do something against her will. Lo Ping had made it plain he would be sticking his nose in where it wasn't wanted.

Not that that had ever stopped him before.

Fargo sighed. His outlook on life had never been live and let live. If he had to sum it up, he would say it was leave-me-be-or-eat-your-teeth.

He chuckled at the notion and it provoked more pain.

Half an hour went by. By then he could think clearly again and move his head without feeling too much discomfort.

The tracks were plain enough. Mai Wing had put up a struggle and dragged her heels until they'd hauled her to where three horses had been tied. She'd been thrown over an animal and they'd headed south.

Fargo did the same. He doubted they would lie in ambush but he kept his hand on his Colt just the same.

Eventually the trees thinned and he came out on a bench that overlooked a winding canyon.

Down the center meandered a stream. On either side the camp had sprung up, a miles-long collection of tents, shacks and cabins, and other buildings. More like a settlement than a camp.

Along the stream, men—all of them Chinese—panned and worked sluice boxes.

Fargo clucked to the Ovaro and descended. He was almost to the mouth of the canyon when he heard the *thunk* of an ax. Rounding a cluster of spruce, he came on a skinny

14

Chinese boy of twelve or so, going at a slim oak with an ax. The boy was terrible at it; he handled the ax as if it were a club.

Drawing rein, Fargo leaned on his saddle horn. "Are you chopping that tree down or beating it to death, boy?"

The skinny kid jumped and turned and nearly tripped over his own feet. He blurted something in Chinese.

"I don't savvy your lingo," Fargo said. "Any chance you speak English?"

The boy set the ax head down and mopped at his sweaty brow with a loose sleeve. "Little bit," he said.

Fargo nodded at the oak. "You're going about it all wrong. Who taught you to use an ax?"

The boy seemed to rack his brain before replying. "No one."

"Could have fooled me." Grunting, Fargo dismounted. He walked over and held out his hand. "How about I show you how it's done?"

Uncertainly, the boy looked at the ax and then gave it to him. "I not good?"

Fargo touched one of the many cuts in the trunk. They were all over the place. Some were inches apart. "You're terrible. It'd take you a month of Sundays at the rate you're going." He motioned. "Stand back." When the boy obeyed, Fargo hefted the ax, and swung, saying, "It needs to go in at an angle. Chop down and then up." He demonstrated, slicing the ax in a downward stroke, pulling it out, and burying it at an upward slant. Chips flew, leaving a V-shaped gash. "See?"

The boy grinned and nodded.

Fargo continued to chop until he was about halfway through, then lowered the ax and held it out. "Your turn."

The boy examined the cut as if it were a revelation. "Chop fast now."

"That's the idea," Fargo said.

A look of determination came over the boy. He spat into his palms, gripped the long handle, and went at the oak again. The ax was almost too heavy but he managed. His first few blows were awkward but he soon settled into a rhythm.

When Fargo gauged the time was right, he said, "Hold on."

Breathing heavily, the boy looked up and arched his eyebrows.

"We give it a push," Fargo said, and placed his hand on the trunk above the cut.

Eagerly, the boy set down the ax and imitated him.

It didn't take much effort. Another cut or three and the oak would have fallen on its own. With a rending crash, the tree toppled, striking the ground with a loud thud. Many of the branches broke and snapped.

Fargo turned to go. "It's all yours."

"Wait," the boy said, and clutched his arm. "I have name."

"No fooling?"

"Yes," The boy tapped his chest. "I Chun," he said. "I chop tree for wood. Sell wood for money."

"Firewood at this time of year?" Fargo said. "Who would use it?"

"Cold in morning," Chun said, and wrapped his arms around himself and shivered. "People make fire."

On second thought, Fargo reflected, the idea wasn't that harebrained. Early mornings were cool in the mountains, and a lot of folks would rather pay for firewood than chop it themselves.

Chun picked up the ax and set to work on the tree.

Fargo debated lending a hand, and turned to the Ovaro. He'd done his good deed for the day and had something more important to do: finding the bastards who damn near caved in his skull. He gripped the reins and the saddle horn and was raising his boot to the stirrups when three men in black came out of the woods.

The boy didn't notice.

They were dressed much like the Hu brothers. All three glanced at Fargo but paid him no more mind than if he were a bug. They came up behind Chun, and as he went to swing the ax, the tallest grabbed the handle and tore it from his grasp.

Startled, the boy turned. He bleated in surprise and fear

and tried to run but the other two sprang and each seized an arm.

To Fargo's amazement, the tall one then backhanded the boy across the face so hard, Chun would have collapsed if not for the pair holding him up.

The tall one angrily barked in Chinese and shook the ax in the boy's face.

The other two smirked in amusement.

Chun said something, and the tall one smacked him again. Chun sagged and drops of blood trickled from a corner of his mouth.

The tall one snarled in Chinese and raised his arm to strike the boy a third time.

By then Fargo was there. He streaked out the Colt and slammed it against the tall man's head and the man folded like an accordion.

Surprise rooted the other two, but only for a few heartbeats. Then they let go of the boy and came at Fargo in a rush. The one on the left aimed a kick at Fargo's knee but he sidestepped.

Shifting, Fargo struck him across the temple with the Colt and sent him staggering.

The third man produced a hatchet from his sleeve.

A gleam of metal out of the corner of his eye gave Fargo an instant's warning. He twisted and the hatchet flashed past his throat. Had it connected, it would have sliced his neck wide. Quick as thought, he smashed the Colt against the man's elbow. The Chinese cried out and recoiled, and Fargo was on him.

The Colt caught the sunlight as the hatchet had done; once, twice, three times, and the man ended up in a crumpled heap.

Chun yelled and pointed.

Fargo whirled. The third man had recovered and drawn a hatchet. Hissing in Chinese, the man sought to bury it in Fargo's chest.

Fargo jerked back, barely in time. He unleashed an uppercut with his left fist and caught the man flush on the chin.

About broke his hand, too, but the blow flattened his attacker like a poled ox.

Just like that, it was over.

Fargo stared at the three still forms, thinking he could have made it easy on himself and simply shot them.

The boy was rooted in astonishment.

"You all right?" Fargo asked.

Chun tore his gaze from the trio and glanced apprehensively at the gold camp. "Bad," he said. "Very bad."

"What is?"

The boy pointed at the men. "Tong."

"Why were they after you?" Fargo wanted to know.

"Ax not mine," the boy said.

"You stole it?"

"I . . . What is word?" Chun scrunched up his grimy face. "I . . . borrow." Unexpectedly, he spun and ran into the forest but stopped to look back and gesture. "Go!" he yelled. "Go far." With that, he disappeared into the undergrowth.

"Well, now," Fargo said. He checked the Colt and twirled it into his holster. He supposed he should take the boy's advice. But his head still hurt, and then there was Mai Wing.

Forking leather, Fargo rode into the camp.

4

Fargo had been in similar gold-or-silver camps before. They sprang up all over. All it took was a few unearthed nuggets or some color in a stream, and the greedy poured in from everywhere to try to get rich quick.

Fargo never had any interest, himself. Dipping a pan into freezing-cold water for hours on end, or picking at rock until blisters broke out, held no appeal. It was hard, back-breaking work, usually with little if any reward.

He preferred the comforts and warmth of a saloon. Give him a friendly poker game and a bottle of Monongahela and a dove on his lap and he was as content as a bull at a feed trough.

And a gold camp like this one was as good a place as any to find all three. Or so he reckoned.

But no. This camp proved to be different.

A sign had been posted at the limits. Instead of English, it bore Chinese characters. Fargo reckoned it identified the place as Hunan. But for all he knew, it might have been a warning for strangers to stay out.

The first thing Fargo noticed was how quiet it was. The usual discordant hubbub of voices and other loud sounds was missing. It was almost as if everyone was going out of their way to be as quiet as they could be.

The streets were narrow and dusty and packed with Chinese. Fargo had seldom seen so many in one place. The last time had been in Chinatown in San Francisco.

He didn't see a single person dressed in Western fash-ion. Their clothes, their hats, their footwear were the same as they'd wear in China. That in itself wasn't odd but how

19

they avoided looking at him was. Those who did glance at him quickly glanced away.

The next thing he noticed was the lack of horses. Usually there would be hitch rails and a lot of mounts tied off. Not here. Nearly all the horses he saw were pulling wagons.

The businesses bore signs—in Chinese.

Here and there Fargo noticed men in black. They were the only ones to stare openly, and there was nothing friendly about the looks they gave him.

He'd gone about a third of the way into the canyon with the stream gurgling on his right when he finally beheld a sign that read GENERAL STORE, and below it another in Chinese.

Reining to the hitch rail, Fargo alighted and stretched.

"As I live and breathe, a white man," a voice boomed, and a stocky man of forty or so, with red hair and ruddy cheeks, came out. He wore an apron and was holding a broom. "As rare as leprechauns, we are."

"Leprechauns?" Fargo said, and grinned.

"A nod to the Old Country," the man said. He leaned the broom against the wall, wiped his hands on his apron, and offered his hand. "Terrence O'Brien is the name, but you can call me Terry. This would be my store, and I welcome you gladly."

"Irish," Fargo said, shaking.

"And proud of it, boyo," O'Brien declared. "I don't give a good damn who hears me say it." He stared up and down the street as if defying anyone to say anything.

Fargo's puzzlement must have shown.

"In these parts," O'Brien said, "those of our persuasion are looked down on by some." He indicated his establishment. "But come on in, why don't you? You must have had a long ride, seeing as how we're so far from anywhere."

Fargo followed him inside. A half dozen or so customers, all Chinese, paid no attention.

The store was neat and clean, the shelves amply stocked. Many of the items were Chinese, with Chinese writing on them. There was a pickle barrel by the counter, and a jar of hard candy.

"Nice place you have," Fargo said by way of small talk.

O'Brien regarded his shelves, and frowned. "I do the best I can, given the circumstances."

"How do you mean?"

"This is Hunan," O'Brien said, as if that were explanation enough.

"Not your usual gold camp?" Fargo fished for information.

"Boyo," O'Brien said gravely, "you don't know the half of it."

A door at the back opened and in walked a pair of women, also wearing aprons. One was O'Brien's age and had her hair pinned back in a bun.

The other interested Fargo more. She was twenty, if that, a winsome beauty with flame red hair and lake blue eyes much like his own. Her complexion, her shape were flawless. She had a natural sway to her hips that Fargo found enticing.

"Who's this, then, Terrence?" asked the older woman.

"He hasn't introduced himself yet, my dear," O'Brien said.

Fargo remedied his lapse.

"These would be my darling wife and daughter," O'Brien then said. "Noirin and I have been married going on twenty-four years. And Flanna, here, is our one and only pride and joy. You'll not find a lovelier lass anywhere."

"Oh, Father," the girl said. She had a soft, husky voice, the kind that sent a tingle through a man clear down to his toes.

"I'm a mite surprised to find you folks here," Fargo mentioned.

It was as if a dark cloud fell. They frowned and looked out the front window.

Noirin recovered first, offering a smile. "Terrence, I trust you've invited Mr. Fargo to supper? It's so rare we have guests these days."

"That it is, my dear," the store owner said, and clasped Fargo's wrist in both big hands. "What do you say, boyo? My wife is the finest cook this side of the Emerald Isle, if I do say so my own self."

"Please say you will, Mr. Fargo," Flanna urged. "We'd be ever so delighted."

Fargo gave them his most charming smile. "Why not?"

"Wonderful," Noirin said gleefully. "I'll start with stew and we'll have colcannon, too. Usually we have them separate but this is a special occasion."

"I can hardly wait, my dear," O'Brien said. To Fargo he said, "We close up here at six. Supper will be at seven."

Fargo had plenty of time to kill. It wasn't even noon yet. "Is there a stable hereabouts?"

"There was," O'Brien said, and the dark cloud fell again. "But the man who ran it closed it up. Not enough business. The Chinese keep their horses out back of the freight company and never did business with him. So he left."

"So they claim," Flanna said.

"Now, now," Noirin said, with a sharp glance at the front door. "Beware of snooping cars."

"I'm not scared of those Oriental devils," Flanna declared.

"Scared of who?" Fargo asked, although he had a notion whom she meant.

O'Brien answered before his daughter could. "Let's just say you should watch yourself while you're here. Hunan, as they call it, isn't like any gold camp you've ever heard of."

"I noticed."

"It's not a camp," Noirin said. "It's a pri—" She looked to one side and caught herself.

A Chinese woman was examining bolts of cloth. From her posture and the way her head was tilted toward them, it was obvious she had been eavesdropping.

"Let's save the talk for supper," O'Brien said quietly to his wife, "or we might scare Mr. Fargo off."

"I wouldn't want that," Flanna said.

It took all of Fargo's self-control not to ogle her in front of her parents.

"Say, I have an idea," Flanna went on. "How about if I give Mr. Fargo a tour? I'll show him where we live and some of the sights."

"I don't know," Noirin said.

"So long as you watch yourself, you hear?" O'Brien said.

"I doubt they'll do anything. Not when they still need me. But you never know."

"I'll avoid them like the plague," Flanna promised.

Fargo said, "Is it me or do you always talk in riddles?"

"All will be made clear soon enough," Flanna responded. She removed her apron, folded it, and set it on the counter. "We won't be long. An hour at the most."

Fargo was hoping for more time in her company. He held the front door open and they watched the ebb and flow of people and wagons.

"God, I hate it here," Flanna remarked out of the blue.

"Then why do you stay?"

"Because my parents can't leave and I refuse to abandon them."

"What's to stop them from closing down and opening a new store somewhere else?"

"We'll tell you about that tonight, I expect."

Flanna made off up the street and he went with her. Staying close to the buildings, she constantly craned her neck to see over the people.

"Looking for someone?"

"To avoid someone is more like it," Flanna responded. "Hunan isn't healthy for our kind."

"By our kind you mean white?"

Flanna shook her head. "By our kind I mean Americans."

"Last I looked at a map," Fargo said, "Utah Territory was part of the United States."

"The man who runs Hunan doesn't see it that way."

Flanna opened her mouth to say more, and froze.

Two Chinese in black were strolling down the middle of the street toward them.

Moving into a gap between a building and a tent, Flanna beckoned.

Fargo stood in front of her so he blocked the view of anyone who passed by. "Why are you hiding?"

"I like to think of it as playing things safe," Flanna said. "There have been a few incidents. I'd like to avoid another." Rising onto her toes, she peered over his shoulder.

23

The pair in black were going by. Neither had noticed her.

"If you know what's good for you," Flanna said anxiously, "you'll avoid anyone who looks and dresses like those two."

Fargo refrained from mentioning his two previous run-ins. "Why should I do that?"

"Because if you're not as careful as can be," Flanna said, "there's a good chance you won't leave this camp alive."

5

Fargo was going to ask her to explain but he saw Lo Ping and an elderly Chinese man emerge from a long building that flanked the stream.

Lo Ping looked mad. He poked the oldster in the chest and gave him a tongue-lashing and the old man stood there and took it, his head bowed, his hands folded at his waist.

"What do you see that interests you so much?" Flanna O'Brien asked, her shoulder brushing his. "Oh. That so-and-so."

"You don't sound very fond of him."

"If I thought I'd get away with it," Flanna said, "I'd slit his damn throat." She paused. "How is it you know Lo Ping?"

"I ran into him earlier," Fargo said, and let it go at that.

"I'm surprised he didn't try to convince you it was in your best interests to stay away from Hunan."

"He did."

"Yet you're still here?" Flanna placed her hand on his arm. "I admire grit, as they call it in this country. But there's a lot to be said for prudence."

"And for not beating around the bush."

Flanna bit her lower lip. "I suppose I am, at that. With good cause. My parents will explain everything tonight." She brightened and looped her arm with his. "Why don't I give you that tour?"

Fargo was more interested in her than in Hunan. She was lively and bright and had a body he would love to explore.

Her tour was instructive. In addition to the prevalence of Chinese, the camp was different in other respects. There were no saloons, which shocked him, but there were gambling

dens, where the Chinese played games of chance like those in China.

"Does that mean whiskey is hard to come by?" Fargo keenly wanted to learn.

"I'm afraid so," Flanna said. "Rice wine is what most of the Chinese drink."

"God," Fargo said.

"The high and mighty Master Han, as they call him, likes everything to be Chinese. Chinese clothes, Chinese food, Chinese drink. Whiskey is considered an American vice, and frowned on."

"I'll have to have a talk with him," Fargo half joked.

Flanna gripped his arm so tight, her nails dug into his flesh. "You don't want to do that. Not unless you're fond of baiting a rattlesnake in its den."

They passed businesses with Chinese signs that sold Chinese goods. They passed a barbershop that was boarded over. They passed a blacksmith's shop, the door open but the interior quiet and still.

They were near a bend in the canyon when Flanna slowed and started to turn as if to go back but must have changed her mind because she said, "You need to see it all."

In a few moments the high canyon walls resounded to hammering and the sounds of saws biting into wood.

Fargo reckoned a building was being constructed but he never in a million years would have guessed what kind. Ahead loomed a structure unlike any other in the camp. It reminded him of buildings he'd seen in Chinatown. Already it was several stories high, and rising, the workers swarming over it like ants.

"Han's Pagoda," Flanna informed him. "It's where he lives. When it's done it will be the tallest building for a thousand miles. Or so Han likes to boast." She motioned. "And what do you think of that?"

A bridge had been built over the stream. Directly across from the Pagoda stood another Chinese structure, three stories high, with ornate carvings and inclined roofs.

"A gambling den?"

"Not quite," Flanna said, and her cheeks grew pink. "It's Madame Lotus's House of Pleasure."

Fargo recollected the madame's name from his talk with Mai Wing. He wondered if that was where she had been brought.

"Hunan's very own house of ill repute," Flanna was saying. "It says something that it's one of the first buildings Han had built."

"Have you been inside?"

Flanna gave him a withering look. "Please. I wouldn't be caught dead in there."

Just then five Chinese men in black came out of the House of Pleasure. Smiling and laughing, they walked to the bridge.

"More of those damnable Tong," Flanna said. "Killers, every one of them. They carry hatchets and aren't shy about using them. Take my advice and stay away from them if you can help it."

A little late for that, Fargo almost said.

"Think of Han as a king and the Tong as the power behind the throne and you'll have a good grasp of the situation," Flanna said angrily.

"Where do you and your family fit in?"

"Us?" Flanna said, venom in her tone. "We're the peasants."

"This isn't China," Fargo said. "No one has the right to lord it over anyone else."

"Someone forgot to tell Han. He does as he pleases. Another year, and Hunan will be his, bottom to top. You've never met anyone like him."

Fargo doubted it. He'd met all kinds in his wide-flung travels.

"He was friendly when we first arrived. The nicest person you'd ever want to meet. Little did we know it was all an act. He was playing us and every other white for dunces."

"I get the idea you don't like him," Fargo joked.

"I *hate* him," Flanna said emphatically. "He's to blame for the deaths and the disappearances. I'm sure of it."

"Who died and disappeared?"

"Father will tell you all about it tonight," Flanna said, yet again. She tugged at his sleeve. "Come. Let's go back."

Fargo turned, and stopped short.

Lo Ping was a few yards away, regarding them with eyes of ice. "What do we have here?" he said cordially. "The man who interferes where he has no business interfering and the woman who doesn't know what is best for her."

"Go to hell, Lo," Flanna said.

To Fargo's surprise, the Chinese man smiled.

"I do not believe in your silly Christian afterlife, Miss O'Brien. When I die it will be the end of me."

"Thank God," Flanna said.

Lo Ping's smile widened. "No wonder the great one is interested in you. You have a fine wit for one of your kind."

"For a woman, you mean?" Flanna said.

All Lo Ping did was smile.

Fargo cut in with, "Where do I find the Hu brothers?"

"Why would you want to do that?" Lo Ping rejoined.

Touching the side of his head, Fargo said, "I owe them something."

Lo Ping chuckled. "I cannot think of anything more foolish. You do not know when you are well off, as the saying here goes. You were given a warning and were too stupid to take it."

Now it was Fargo who indulged in an icy smile. "They're not the only ones I've been looking for."

"Oh?"

Fargo balled his fists and took a half step and Lo Ping flinched and took a step back.

"You wouldn't."

"You put them up to jumping me, you son of a bitch."

Lo Ping fearfully gestured. "All I have to do is yell and there will be a dozen Tong here, just like that." He snapped his fingers. "If you don't believe me, ask Miss O'Brien."

"By the time they got here," Fargo said, "you'd be spitting teeth."

"I warn you, American," Lo Ping said. "Harm me and it

28

is the same as harming my master. He would take it as an insult."

"Ask me if I give a damn."

"You would if you have a shred of intellect." Lo Ping did a surprising thing; he spread his arms wide and said, "But go ahead. Hit me if you want. I will not resist."

Fargo almost did.

Lo Ping waited, and said, "So. You are not entirely reckless. It is good to know the strengths and weaknesses of one's enemies."

"You think awful highly of yourself."

The comment seemed to perplex Lo Ping. "Why should I behave as man at his worst? Or is it that you expect us to be as simpleminded as ordinary American thugs?" Lo Ping grinned. "You underestimate us if that is the case."

He placed his hands in his sleeves and bowed. "But I have things to do for my master. We will talk again, I am sure. And, Miss O'Brien, I can't say my master will be pleased by the company you keep." He smiled and walked around them toward the Pagoda.

"That weasel could talk rings around a tree," Fargo said in disgust.

"Make no mistake," Flanna said. "He's dangerous and he's devious. But he's not half as vile as Han." She clutched his wrist. "Please. Let's get out of here. Han might send his hatchet men to take you to him."

"I'd like to see them try," Fargo said. But he went with her, his mind awhirl with all he'd learned. It begged the question: How deeply did he want to get involved? Because if he kept at it, there would be gunplay and a lot of people would die.

Flanna misconstrued his thoughtfulness. "It's hard to believe, isn't it? A slice of China here in the middle of nowhere?"

"It's smart of Han," Fargo said. "There's no law except the federal marshals and it could be years before one happens by."

"And what would a lawman find even if he came?"

Flanna said. "A quiet, orderly community. He'd ride in and ride out again with no idea of the evil of the place." She shuddered slightly. "My parents have talked about sending for the army. But what good would that do? The army doesn't involve itself in civilian matters. Unless Han intends to overthrow the government, they'd have no cause to take him into custody."

The more Fargo learned, the more he hankered to set eyes on this "Master Han."

"No," Flanna said, "we're on our own. So far Han hasn't driven us off or given the order to have us killed. But he'll get around to it eventually." She suddenly stopped. "What's this?"

Fargo looked up.

The three Tong who had assaulted the boy were blocking their way. All three bore bruises from his pistol, and one had a badly swollen jaw.

The tall one hissed in Chinese.

"Miss me?" Fargo taunted.

The tall one slipped a hand under his shirt and drew out a hatchet.

6

Fargo swooped his hand to his Colt but to his consternation Flanna O'Brien stepped between them. She said a few words in Chinese—the only one Fargo understood was "Han"— and pointed at the Pagoda.

The tall Tong hesitated. His eyes narrowed and he growled at her and she calmly replied. With what must have been an oath, he replaced the hatchet and angrily strode around them, his two glaring companions in tow.

"You savvy Chinese?" Fargo said when the trio were out of hatchet-throwing range.

"Not really," Flanna said. "Only a few words. Enough to remind Nan Kua that Mr. Han might not like him spilling blood."

"It would have been his blood that was spilled," Fargo assured her.

"Even worse," Flanna said, "for then Han might decree that you must die."

"Decree?" Fargo said. "You make him sound like a king."

"He practically is. Haven't I made it plain by now that Han rules this camp? His every wish, his every whim are blindly followed."

"The other Chinese like him that much?"

"They live in fear of him and his Tong," Flanna replied. She gazed out over the men panning the stream and the people in the street. "The other Chinese are nice as can be. If not for Han everyone would get along fine."

As if to prove her point, an older couple walking by both smiled and the man said politely in English, "How do you do, Miss O'Brien?"

"Fine, thank you," Flanna responded. Lowering her voice, she said in Fargo's ear, "Those bruises on Nan Kua and his friends. Was that your doing?"

Fargo nodded.

"Come on, then." Flanna took his hand and hurried up the street. "Nan Kua will likely run to Lo Ping and Lo Ping will go to Master Han, and then you'll be in Tong up to your neck."

Fargo let her lead him. He wouldn't run from a fight but he wouldn't provoke one, either. Not until he was ready.

As they came abreast of the blacksmith's, Fargo heard the metallic ring of a hammer on metal.

"Hold up," Flanna said, and went in.

A brawny man of middle years with a bald head but a bushy mustache was hammering a horseshoe on an anvil. He was naked from the waist up, and his muscles rippled as he swung. He was so intent on his work that he didn't notice them until Flanna nudged his arm.

Instantly the blacksmith spun and raised his hammer as if to strike. "Miss O'Brien!" he blurted, and lowered it again. "You shouldn't sneak up on a man like that."

"This is a friend, Skye Fargo," Flanna said, introducing him. "Skye, this is Tom Bannon."

"A white man, by God," Bannon declared. He set the hammer on the anvil and offered his callused hand. "Welcome to hell."

Flanna asked, "What's this my father tells me about you leaving?"

Bannon nodded. "I've had it. I'm sick of Han and his bullies. I don't care how much he pays me. I'm sneaking out of here." He gestured at the anvil. "I'm shoeing my horse right now, in fact."

"Does Han know?" Flanna asked.

"The only one I've told is your pa," the blacksmith said.

"What about your tools? Your anvil?"

"I've got a buckboard," Bannon said.

Fargo wasn't sure he'd heard right. "You're fixing to sneak off in a wagon?"

"I know what you're thinking," Bannon said. "I'll wait

until the middle of the night. Hardly anyone is ever up and about."

"You're taking an awful risk," Flanna said.

"I don't care. There's only so much a man can abide. I was a fool to agree to stay." Bannon added as an afterthought, "And a greedy fool at that."

"You'll say good-bye before you go?"

"Need you ask? You and your family are the best friends I have here." Bannon turned back to the anvil, picked up his hammer, and resumed pounding on the horseshoe.

Flanna sighed and went back out. "I'll be sorry to see him go. We always knew we could count on him if push came to shove."

"What was that about greed?"

"A common condition," Flanna said. "In Tom's case, he was all set to pack up and leave when Han made him an offer he couldn't say no to. Tom's the only blacksmith and Han needed him." She wrung her hands. "I hope he gets away without a hitch."

"How about you?"

"I won't leave if my parents don't. It's entirely up to them."

"Not that," Fargo said. "Who do you cuddle with at night?"

Flanna stopped as if she had walked into a wall. Her mouth fell and she began to laugh but stopped. "Wait. You're serious?"

"A body as fine as yours," Fargo said, "it would be a shame to let it go to waste."

"My word," Flanna said.

"I wouldn't mind paying you a visit after your folks have turned in."

A pink tinge crept into Flanna's cheeks. "Oh, you wouldn't, would you?" Facing him, she poked him in the chest. "My parents have done you the honor of inviting you for a meal and you talk to me as if I'm a common trollop?"

"There's nothing common about you," Fargo said. From her hair to her toes she had as fine a figure as he'd ever laid eyes on.

"I refuse to be addressed in this manner." Her spine as straight as a board, Flanna wheeled and stalked off.

Fargo quickly caught up. "Do you always get mad when someone says you're good-looking?"

"You said more than that," Flanna said. "You made it sound as if you want to ravish me."

Fargo smiled. "I do."

Flabbergasted, Flanna broke her stride, recovered, and stormed on.

Fargo easily kept pace. "You're even prettier when your dander is up."

"Don't talk to me."

"Your folks must coddle you."

Digging in her heels, Flanna wheeled on him. Her eyes were smoldering pits. *"Coddle . . . me?"*

"Protect you. Keep their little darling safe from the wolves of the world."

The pink in her cheeks became scarlet from her neckline to her hairline. "I have half a mind to sock you in the mouth."

"I'd sock back," Fargo said.

"You're despicable."

"I wasn't rude. I didn't take liberties. Despicable hardly fits."

"You said you want to make love to me. What else would you call it?"

"About the highest compliment a man can give a woman."

Flanna blinked. "I never."

"Then it's about time," Fargo said.

"No. I didn't mean I hadn't ever—" Flanna caught herself and the red became practically purple. "You're twisting my words. You have me so tongue-tied, I don't know what I'm saying."

"I'd rather suck on it than tie it."

Flanna put her hands on her hips and threw back her head and laughed. "I understand now. You're saying all this for humor's sake."

"No," Fargo said. "I'm saying it because I'd like to see you without clothes on."

Flanna raised a hand to her throat. "You can't just come out with it!"

"Why not?"

"How did we get on this subject? I'm so confused, my head is spinning."

"Could be it's not confusion," Fargo said. "Could be you're excited."

Flanna pivoted on a heel. "Leave me alone. I don't want to talk to you anymore." She pumped her long legs energetically.

Fargo's legs were longer. As he overtook her he admired the saucy sway to her hips. "One kiss would prove me right or wrong."

"No."

"What can it hurt?"

"It'll hurt you when I knock your teeth out," Flanna said.

"It would be worth it."

"Go away."

"I've been invited to supper, remember?"

"Which isn't for hours yet. I'd rather not see you until then." Flanna walked faster.

So did Fargo.

So fast, some of the people they passed cast curious looks.

"I don't know how I could have been so mistaken about you. I took you for a gentleman."

"When was the last time you kissed a man?"

"That's none of your damn business."

"Oh my," Fargo mimicked her. "Such language. I took you for a lady."

"I wouldn't kiss you now if you were the last man on earth."

"Good thing I'm not then."

Flanna stopped and turned with her hands balled into fists. "One more word, and so help me."

Fargo grinned and held his hands up, palms out, to show he was harmless. Then he leaned in close and kissed her on the mouth.

Flanna tensed. Her fists began to rise.

For a few seconds Fargo thought he had gone too far and she would carry out her threat to slug him. He let his lips linger, lightly, and when her fists stopped rising, he drew back and smiled. "Thank you. That was nice."

Flanna sputtered.

"There's more where that came from if you're of a mind," Fargo said, and before she could collect her wits, he headed off.

Now it was Flanna's turn to catch up to him. "I think I hate you."

"Could be it's not hate," Fargo teased. "Could be it's love."

"No, no thinking about it," Flanna said. "I definitely hate you."

"You say you do but your lips said you don't."

"That makes no sense at all."

Fargo shrugged. "We'll find out tonight after your folks turn in."

"And what do you think is going to happen?"

"You," Fargo said, "will ravish me."

7

Flanna barely spoke to him the rest of the way to the general store. He left her at the front door and was about to climb on the Ovaro when he noticed an old man who came out of the long, low building with two women. It was the same old man Lo Ping had been angry with.

Something about the women struck him as peculiar: the way they looked, the way they moved.

Forking leather, Fargo crossed at a point where the stream narrowed. There was no hitch rail so he let the reins dangle and went to the door. Signs in Chinese told him absolutely nothing.

Fargo pushed on the door, and right away knew it was an opium den. The smell, for one thing. The smoke and the haze, for another.

The old man was seated on a low stool, a quill pen in hand, writing Chinese characters on a parchment. He looked up and smiled and said a few words in Chinese.

Fargo entered. He reckoned he might as well see it all. "Savvy English?" he asked.

The old man tilted his head and answered in Chinese. He smiled, revealing a mouth full of yellow teeth. His face was as wrinkled as a prune and as pale as a bedsheet. His beard, which hung halfway to his waist, was neatly trimmed. His eyes were alert enough but betrayed a trace of an addiction.

Fargo had to stoop to enter. The doorway was too low for someone his size. Inside, it was as cramped as a prairie dog den. Here and there lamps broke the shadows, illuminating ogre faces.

37

The old man rose and bowed.

Fargo imitated holding a long pipe stem and puffing on it.

Smiling, the old man motioned and led him into the warren.

Fargo's gut churned in revulsion. He had been in opium dens a few times before. Give him whiskey any day.

The patrons were exclusively Chinese. Men and women of all ages were adrift in the bliss induced by the narcotic. Most lay on narrow cots covered with blankets or sat with their backs to a wall. Some smiled blankly at him. Others were so far lost in their own little worlds, they had no idea he was there.

The old man prattled as they went. As near as Fargo could tell, he was pointing out the finer points of his establishment.

Fargo didn't go all the way in. Fifty feet or so was enough. His hunch had been right. He tapped the old man on the shoulder and shook his head. "No, thanks," he said. "I'd rather be drunk."

His spurs jangling, Fargo went back out. He breathed mouthfuls of fresh air, climbed on the Ovaro, and headed deeper into the camp.

Most of the Chinese studiously avoided looking at him. Except for the Tong. Here and there he saw men in black and they always glared. He imagined word had spread about him. But apparently they were under orders not to bother him because they left him alone.

The House of Pleasure was a wonderment. The Chinese architecture, the finely wrought detail in the carvings, the gables, the place was a work of art.

Surprisingly enough, a hitch rail had been provided. Fargo no sooner dismounted and took a step than a pair of grinning young women in tight dresses came out and attached themselves to his elbows.

"Ladies," he said grandly, smiling, "you must be the greeters."

They giggled and shook their heads to signify they didn't savvy.

"Would Madame Lotus happen to be in?" Fargo asked, knowing full well they couldn't answer.

"I am always in," said a husky voice with a lilting accent.

She was a stunner. Her age was hard to guess but Fargo pegged it as thirty to forty. She wore an exquisite Chinese dress. Her hair, her face, her nails were immaculate. She reminded him of one of those little Chinese dolls sold in Chinatown, brought to life. Her teeth, when she smiled, were flawless.

"Madame Lotus, I reckon," Fargo stated the obvious.

She smiled and bowed and snapped at the two girls, who bowed their heads and stepped away.

"I don't stink that bad," Fargo said.

Madame Lotus's delicate nose crinkled in amusement. "It is not that," she said politely. "I will escort you personally."

"I'm flattered."

"You should be." Madame Lotus took him by the right elbow but he lifted her hand off and lightly pulled her around to the left side.

She was sharp; she glanced at the Colt on his right hip and her smile widened. But she didn't say anything other than, "You have heard of the delights of my House, perhaps, and would like to taste of them for yourself?"

"I'd like a look-see," Fargo said. "It's early in the day yet and I usually do my poking at night." Which was a bald-faced lie. He'd make love any hour of the day or night.

"I would be most honored to show you around," Madame Lotus said courteously.

It was like entering another world. Or stepping across the Pacific Ocean into China. Everything was Chinese. By any standards, her whorehouse was luxurious. The furnishings, the decorations, had been brought all the way from the mother country.

A fragrant scent tingled Fargo's nose. To the right was a parlor where more than a dozen brightly dressed young women sat primly awaiting gentlemen callers. Their painted faces, their rouge, they were more China dolls.

"If you should see a lady you like," Madame Lotus said, "you will find it is never too early for pillow talk."

Her melodious voice stirred Fargo where he had no intention of being stirred. "How about you?"

"I beg your pardon?"

"Is it ever too early for you?"

Madame Lotus's eyes widened slightly, and she laughed. "Oh. That can never be. I do not offer myself. I must reserve my affections for someone special."

Fargo could guess whom. "That's a shame," he said with forced regret. "I'd give you a poke here and now."

She was pleased by his flattery but tried to hide it. "I am most sorry that I am not available. We have dozens of other ladies for you to choose from."

The hallway was as elegant as the parlor. Everywhere a feast for the eyes. A turn took them into another corridor where the walls were made of rice paper.

Fargo stopped and touched the wall on the right. The paper was smooth to the touch, and thinner than he would have thought.

"Beautiful, is it not?" Madame Lotus said proudly. "My master spared no expense in building the House of Pleasure."

"It's different," Fargo said.

"Would you like to see one of the rooms?" Madame Lotus moved to a section of wall that was actually a partition. She slid it aside, revealing a middling-sized room bare of furniture save for a mat and pillows and a small table with a teapot and accessories.

"Kind of plain," Fargo said.

Madame Lotus entered and motioned. "But functional. One can focus on the pleasure of the senses and not be distracted."

"Is that so?" Fargo said. Boldly walking up to her, he cupped her bottom and drew her against him. "Why don't you show me?"

Madame Lotus smiled and calmly said, "I told you before. I am not to be paid for."

"That's too bad," Fargo said, and kissed her. "You'd likely curl a man's tocs."

Her mouth formed a delightful oval and she gently pushed him away. "I must ask you to behave."

"I'll try," Fargo said.

She led him back out and closed the partition. "Now that you have seen what we have to offer, may I expect you this evening?"

"You never know."

Suddenly, from the bowels of the building, a faint, fluttering scream wavered. Fargo heard it clearly, and glanced in the direction it came from. "What was that?"

"What was what?"

"You didn't hear it? It sounded like a woman in pain."

Madame Lotus smiled. "This is the House of Pleasure. Some of our customers derive their pleasure *from* pain."

"Whips and rope?" Fargo said.

"Whatever our customer requires," Madame Lotus said. "Their happiness is our paramount duty."

Fargo suspected there was more to it than that. He had half a mind to go find the screamer. But he let Madame Lotus usher him along the hall to the parlor. "I'm obliged for the tour."

"It was my delight," Madame Lotus said.

Fargo turned to go, and stopped.

Nan Kua and the two Tong with bruised faces had just walked in. Nan Kua gave a start and said something to the others. All three glared.

Madame Lotus smiled and addressed them in Chinese. Whatever Nan Kua snarled in reply brought a look of dismay.

"Oh my," she said.

"What is it?" Fargo asked, casually resting his right hand on his Colt.

"It appears that these three have been looking for you," Madame Lotus said.

"Some jackasses never learn," Fargo said.

Nan Kua spat more Chinese at Madame Lotus. Her dismay deepened.

"I am to tell you that you have been invited to Master

Han's Pagoda. Nan Kua and his friends are to escort you there."

"No," Fargo said.

"You do not understand," Madame Lotus said. "You must go with them. An invitation from Master Han is the same as a command."

"For you, maybe," Fargo said. "I couldn't give a good damn."

Nan Kua evidently asked what they were saying and Madame Lotus translated. Fury crackled on the tall Tong's brow, and he barked at her.

"I am afraid you have no choice. Nan Kua says you are to go with them whether you want to or not."

"And if I don't want to?"

"Please. Why are you being so unreasonable?"

"Unreasonable, hell. I'm free to do as I damn well please."

"I am most sorry," Madame Lotus said, "but he says that if you refuse to go of your own free will, they will force you."

"Let them try," Fargo said.

8

Nan Kua snarled at Madame Lotus, apparently asking her what Fargo had said. Wringing her slender hands, she translated.

Fargo thought he was ready. His fingers were curled around the Colt and he was poised to draw. He figured Nan Kua would say something to the other two and all three would come at him at once.

He was wrong.

Without another word, without any forewarning, Nan Kua sprang. He took a step and leaped into the air, his left foot extended.

Instinctively, Fargo swept his right arm up to block the kick. He succeeded, but the impact knocked him back.

Before he could set himself, Nan Kua spun, his other leg sweeping out.

Fargo ducked, and lost his hat.

Since Nan Kua hadn't resorted to a weapon, Fargo didn't either. Cocking his fists, he waded into the tall Tong. Nan Kua chopped at his neck and he sidestepped and let fly with a solid cross that rocked Nan Kua onto his heels.

The other two rushed in.

Fargo backpedaled into the parlor, where there was more room to move.

The women jumped to their feet, several crying out in alarm, and moved to get out of the way.

The other two Tong came after him. They didn't rely on weapons, either; they rushed in with a flurry of hands and feet.

A sandal arced at Fargo's face. Twisting, he buried his

knuckles in the man's ribs. The Tong grunted and sagged. The other one slipped in and thrust the tips of his fingers at Fargo's throat but Fargo dodged and smashed him in the mouth.

The Chinese doubled over. The other one was sinking to the floor.

Fargo drew back his leg to kick—and glimpsed movement out of the corner of his eye.

Nan Kua was coming at him again, and this time he had his hatchet.

Barely avoiding a slash at his chest, Fargo gripped Nan Kua's wrist to prevent him from swinging again.

Nan Kua whipped around, seeking to throw him off, but he held on and brought his bootheel down as hard he could on Nan Kua's left sandal—onto his toes.

A shriek ripped from Nan Kua's throat and he staggered.

Quickly, Fargo swept his foot under Nan Kua's other leg, the leg shot out from under, and Fargo slammed him to the floor. The ax went skittering. Nan Kua lunged at Fargo's throat, his fingers rigid, and Fargo punched him. Not once, but four times, as hard as he could on the point of Nan Kua's chin.

The other two were getting back to their feet.

In a twinkling Fargo had the Colt out and brought the barrel crashing down on the head of the first. Swiveling, he delivered a bone-jarring blow to the last man's jaw.

In the abrupt stillness, Fargo heard one of the China dolls gasp.

Holstering the Colt, Fargo rubbed his knuckles.

"You defeated them," Madame Lotus said, sounding amazed that he had.

"They're not so tough," Fargo said, when, in fact, they were.

"Three Tong, by yourself," Madame Lotus said. "I have never seen that done."

Fargo turned toward the entrance. Where there were three Tong there may be more.

"Wait, please," Madame Lotus said, and reaching out,

she cupped his chin. She turned his head to one side and then the other, studying him as if he were a mystery. "How is it you prevailed? What manner of man are you?"

"A hungry one," Fargo said. But it would be hours yet before he sat down at the supper table with the O'Briens. His stomach rumbled at the prospect.

"You are remarkable," Madame Lotus said. "The Tong are formidable fighters."

Some of the girls were whispering. Fargo smiled at them and stepped over the last man he'd felled. "Might see you again," he mentioned.

"I sincerely hope so," Madame Lotus said. "I have not met a man in a very long time who interests me as much as you do."

"I'll interest you more with my clothes off," Fargo said.

Madame Lotus laughed. "I do so look forward to your next visit. You are highly entertaining."

Nan Kua groaned.

Fargo touched his hat brim and got out of there. The harsh glare of the sun made him squint as he climbed on the Ovaro and reined to the west. He rode clear to the end of the canyon and on out into the forest beyond. When he had gone far enough that he was sure not to be disturbed, he stopped at the first clearing he came to, gathered firewood, and put coffee on to brew.

Fargo had a decision to make. He could ride on, forget about Han and the O'Briens and Mai Wing and go on about his own business. That was the thing to do if he had a shred of common sense.

But then there was Flanna and her ripe body, Madame Lotus and her carnal delights, maybe even Mai Wing if he played his cards right.

"Hell," Fargo said. It wouldn't surprise him if his pecker got him killed someday. A woman once called him a buck in perpetual rut, and that was as good a description as any.

When the coffee was hot enough he filled his cup and sat back. He had to remind himself that Han wasn't breaking any laws. Whorehouses weren't illegal, not in Utah Territory, anyway. Nor were opium dens.

He should skedaddle. He should finish his coffee and climb on the Ovaro and go wherever the wind took him. He should forget everything that had happened and leave the gold camp to Han and the Tong.

Instead, he sat and drank and relaxed as the sun crawled across the vault of blue. When it was about to disappear below the horizon he was on his way back to Hunan.

A lot fewer people were abroad. The nightlife wasn't as lusty and rowdy as most gold camps.

During their walk Flanna had pointed out where her family lived, and as the gray of twilight spread along the canyon floor, Fargo drew rein in front of their house. A simple frame affair, it boasted a small fenced yard with a few flowers and a porch with the inevitable rocking chair.

Fargo tied the Ovaro and went to the door and knocked. He didn't know what sort of reception he'd receive. Flanna might have told her parents his antics and they could well refuse to let him in.

Flanna herself opened the door.

Fargo braced for a tongue-lashing but she smiled and held out her hand and touched his arm.

"So you made it? Good. We were worried you might not. Come on in."

"You're looking as gorgeous as always," Fargo remarked. She had on a different dress that fit so snugly, it accented every contour in her delectable body. It also, to his surprise, showed some cleavage. Either her folks were more open-minded than a lot of parents or she was being brazen.

The house was simply but comfortably furnished. Flanna escorted him to the parlor and bid him take a seat on a settee. He barely sank down when Terrence and Noirin O'Brien entered. Both wore smiles and greeted him warmly.

"We were worried for your safety, boyo," the storekeeper said. "There's a rumor sweeping the camp that you tangled with the Tong."

"I did," Fargo confirmed.

The parents swapped looks.

"That's not good," Terrence said. "No one ever stands up to them and gets away with it. They're vengeful bastards."

"Terry," Noirin said. "Your language, if you please."

"Sorry, love," Terry responded. "But you know how the Tong make my blood boil."

"Let's save that for later, shall we?" Noirin suggested. "After we've eaten."

Terry grumbled but let it drop.

Over the next half an hour Fargo was treated to small talk about life in the gold camp and in Ireland before the family came to America. Flanna was strangely subdued and sat quietly with her hands in her lap.

The meal, as Mrs. O'Brien had said it would be, was pure Irish. Her stew was delicious. Fargo had never had colcannon before, and liked it. For dessert there was a dish called apple duff. Fargo wasn't much for sweets but had a second helping.

Afterward, Terry O'Brien patted his belly in contentment. "Was I right about my one true love being the best cook this side of the Emerald Isle?"

"I've never tasted better," Fargo said.

"You flatter me," Noirin said, clearly pleased.

Terry produced a cigar. He offered one to Fargo but Fargo declined. Terry used a lucifer to light it and puffed until the tip gave off plumes of smoke. Sitting back, he said to his wife, "I suppose we should get to it, then."

Noirin nodded and turned to Fargo. "I hope you won't hold it against us, but we had a secret motive for inviting you here."

"It wasn't for my company?"

Noirin blushed and said quickly, "There was that, too. But—" She stopped. "You're teasing me, aren't you?"

"Get on with it, dear," Terry said. "Or would you rather I do the honors?"

"You," Noirin said. "He might be more open, hearing it man to man, as they say."

Terry blew a smoke ring at the ceiling, and frowned. "I don't need to go into detail about the situation here. You're well aware of it. Han holds this camp in a fist of iron, and rules through the Tong. Dare defy him and he sets his hatchet men on you." He paused. "Han has made it clear whites

47

aren't welcome. Tom Bannon and us are about the last. Tom leaves tonight."

Noirin chimed in with, "We would very much like to go with him. But there's our store, you see. All our stock. We plan to stop ordering merchandise and sell off most of what we have and then slip away in the dead of night as Tom is doing. But that will take weeks if not months."

Terry nodded. "We don't mind risking our own lives but it would ease our minds considerably if our daughter was safe. So I'd like to ask you, man to man, as my wife put it, if you'd be willing to do us a favor?"

Fargo looked at Flanna. At her cleavage. "Let me guess," he said.

"When you leave," Terrence O'Brien said, "we would very much like for you to take her with you."

9

Fargo half expected Flanna to object. She didn't. She sat in her chair with her head bowed and a faint pink blush to her cheeks.

"We realize we hardly know you," Terry went on, "but with you she has a chance of making it out of the mountains alive."

Fargo brought up the obvious. "Why not have her go with Bannon?"

Noirin said, "We had that very idea when he first confided in us that he was leaving." She gave her daughter a troubled glance. "But Flanna refuses to go with him and won't say why."

"Contrariness, if you ask me," Terry declared. "She thinks her proper place is at our side."

"It is," Flanna broke her silence.

"We appreciate that, girl," Terry said. "We truly do. It's a fine lass you are, to hold your parents in such high regard."

"But every day we live in fear for your safety," Noirin said. "With you gone, we could breathe easier."

"Who are you trying to fool, Mother?" Flanna responded. "It will make Han mad. He's liable to do anything."

"Posh," Noirin said. "He won't harm us. He relies on our store for things he needs."

"Only until he opens a store of his own," Flanna said. "Word is he's sent for a Chinese merchant who will run a store controlled by Han."

"Be that as it may," Terry said, "we want you out of this infernal camp, and that's final." He turned to Fargo. "So will you or won't you?"

"You could leave this very night," Noirin said. "The same as Tom Bannon. Let him go his way and you go yours. Han might think that you went with him and send the Tong after him. It would gain you the time to get clean away."

"Mother," Flanna said. "That's a terrible thing to say. It's using Mr. Bannon as bait."

"I like him," Noirin said, "but you're our daughter. Your welfare comes before all else."

Fargo nipped their argument in the bud by saying, "I don't figure to leave for a couple of days yet."

Terry sat up straighter. "What? Why not, in God's name? Why stick around?"

"I'm a prickly cuss."

"What does that mean?" Noirin asked. "It's our daughter's life we're talking about. Whatever reason you have for staying, it can't be more important than she is."

"It doesn't have to be tonight," Terry sought to compromise. "It could be tomorrow night or the next."

"Terrence," Noirin said.

Terry reached over and placed his hand on hers. "The important thing is that he takes her."

"Tonight is best, I tell you," Noirin insisted. Pulling her hand free, she bent across the table toward Fargo. "Would money change your mind?"

"Noirin," Terry said.

She ignored him. "We don't have a lot but what we do have is yours if you'll take Flanna away from here this very night. Two thousand dollars, every penny we've saved, and it's yours."

"Noirin," Terry said again.

Noirin motioned in annoyance. "Hush. I'm trying to strike a bargain with our guest."

"If I take her," Fargo said, "it will be because I want to."

"Now you've done it, woman," Terry said to his wife. "You've gone and insulted him."

"Where's the insult in paying him for his trouble?" Noirin countered. "He knows how much she means to us."

"You're suggesting he has a mercenary nature," Terry said. "Some men wouldn't like that."

"That's pride, that is," Noirin said. "And I won't let pride stand in the way of our daughter being safe and free." Her eyes bored into Fargo's. "What do you say? You could take her to Salt Lake City. It's the nearest town of any size, and civilized. She could find lodgings and wait for us to join her."

"It's overrun with Mormons," Terry said.

"Terrence O'Brien," Noirin scolded. "Since when did you become intolerant of the religion of others? Besides, Salt Lake is to the east and well out of Han's influence. He came here by way of San Francisco, where he still has considerable sway."

Fargo glanced at Flanna. She studiously avoided looking at him. He reckoned it would take a week or better for them to get there. All those nights, alone under the stars. "I might be willing to," he conceded.

"Might isn't good enough," Noirin said. "We need your solemn promise."

"Might is all you get for now," Fargo said.

"We've invited you into our home, we've fed you, and you treat us like this?" Noirin snapped.

Terry pounded the table so hard, the dishes and silverware jumped. "That will be quite enough. Keep this up and he'll refuse to spite you."

"Surely not," Noirin said.

Sighing, Terry gestured at Fargo. "I apologize for my wife. She's distraught. Normally she wouldn't think to impose on anyone."

"Damn it, Terrence," Noirin said.

"As you can see," Terry said with a grin, "between her Irish temper and her stubborn streak, she's a handful."

Fargo pushed his chair back and stood. "I'm obliged for the meal," he said. "If things work out I might be able to take Flanna away before morning. But I can't make any promises."

"We can't ask for more than that," Terry said.

Noirin said, "Sure we can."

Fargo touched his hat brim and went to leave but Flanna said his name.

"If you should decide to take me," she quietly stated,

"I'd be happy to accompany you. I know you'd be a perfect gentleman the whole journey."

Fargo almost snorted. She knew he hankered to have her. He wondered what she was playing at, and replied, "It's rough country. And we'd have to watch out for hostiles."

"I would place myself completely in your hands."

Fargo smiled. There it was, as plain as she could make it with her parents sitting there. "I'm happy to hear that. I'll let you know."

Terry walked him to the front door. "Whether you do or you don't, I can't thank you enough. You've given us our first real hope in months."

"How long before you join her in Salt Lake City?"

"It's difficult to say. We'll have to liquidate on the sly. If Han catches on, our goose is cooked." Terry opened the door and held out his hand. "Take care of yourself, you hear? I don't know what you're up to, but I'd advise you to stay away from the Tong if you can help it."

Fargo couldn't. He went out and Terry closed the door behind him. He walked to the Ovaro and was reaching for the saddle horn when he noticed the stallion's head was up and its ears pricked. He spun but it was too late.

A ring of dark-clad figures had him surrounded.

Fargo streaked his right hand to his Colt. He'd be damned if he'd go down without a fight.

"That will not be necessary," a familiar voice said, and Lo Ping stepped into the circle. His hands up his sleeves, he smiled his insincere smile. "We are not here to harm you."

"Then why?" Fargo demanded.

"My master would like a word with you," Lo Ping said. "Many words, actually."

"Han wants to see me?"

"None other. Why do you sound surprised? After the incident today at the House of Pleasure, and others, it was as inevitable as the rising and setting of the sun."

"You sure do love to hear yourself talk."

If Lo Ping took offense he didn't show it. "You may bring your horse if you like. But walk him. Don't ride."

"If I refuse?"

52

"We are under orders to bring you whether you want to or not and I brought more of us than there are bullets in your six-gun."

Fargo never had liked being bossed around. Whenever someone rode roughshod over him, his natural inclination was to feed them their teeth. Then again . . . "Fact is, I'd like to meet this master of yours."

"You should be honored," Lo Ping said. "Not many are admitted to his celestial presence."

"I've never met a celestial before," Fargo said, taking hold of the reins. "Lead the way."

Men in black closed in on either side.

"Not too close," Fargo warned.

"Every one of these men would love to test his mettle against you," Lo Ping said. "They heard what you did to Nan Kua and the others."

"Like dogs on a leash," Fargo said.

"Oh, our Tong are much more, I assure you," Lo Ping said. "We are a venerable society, older than your country. In our own land we are held in great respect."

"I'd heard it was fear."

"That too," Lo Ping said.

The people who were out and about gave a wide berth to the men in black. Most of the businesses were closed but the opium den was doing brisk trade. So was the House of Pleasure.

"Madame Lotus was given a reprimand, thanks to you," Lo Ping mentioned. "She is fortunate she wasn't punished more severely."

"The fight wasn't her fault."

"The House of Pleasure is her establishment. It is her duty to maintain order."

"Nan Kua started it," Fargo said. He wondered why he was defending her.

"So she informed us. That, too, will be dealt with before too long."

The Pagoda towered above them, an architectural colossus that would rise even higher in the weeks and months ahead. Lights were lit all over.

More Tong stood guard out front. Some had hatchets at their waist. Others, their hatchets were hidden.

"What do you have against guns?" Fargo asked out of curiosity.

"Our own weapons have always served us well," Lo Ping said. "In the Triads in our own country, and now here."

Stepping into the Pagoda was like stepping into China.

Every facet, every article was Chinese: the lamps, the furnishings, the paintings, and the designs. It was like Madame Lotus's, only grander.

Lo Ping led Fargo up a series of stairs. At each landing Fargo gazed down a hall fit for a palace.

At the fifth-floor landing there were more guards.

"These are our master's temporary quarters while the Pagoda is being finished," Lo Ping revealed.

The chamber Fargo was admitted to was the most lavish yet. It included, incredibly, a throne on a raised dais.

And there, waiting for him, sat the gold camp's self-appointed ruler.

"I'll be damned," Fargo said.

10

Fargo didn't know what he expected. The biggest and fiercest of the Tong, maybe. Or a weasel like Lo Ping.

On the throne sat an old man who must have been seventy if he was a day, and more likely older. He looked so small and frail, it was a wonder he could sit up straight. His hair was white, his face shrunken. His thin elbows rested on the arms of his ornate chair and his hands formed a V in front of him. He was smiling a catlike smile.

"*That's* the great Han?" Fargo said without thinking.

"Show respect," Lo Ping growled so only Fargo heard. "All my master has to do is snap his finger and you will be chopped to pieces."

The choppers, Fargo saw, were fourteen more Tong who stood alertly along the walls. By their expressions, they, too, wouldn't mind testing his mettle.

Lo Ping took a couple of steps, and bowed. "Great one," he called out. "I bring he whom you requested."

One of Han's slim fingers moved, and Lo Ping motioned at Fargo and escorted him across the spacious chamber. The floor was polished wood, the ceiling crisscrossed by large timbers.

Fargo stopped when Lo Ping did.

Lo Ping addressed his lord and master in Chinese.

"We will speak the American's language, if you please," Han said in impeccable English. His dark eyes fixed on Fargo with startling intensity. "So you are the one I have heard so much about."

Lo Ping was doubled at the waist, and said out of the corner of his mouth, "Bow to my master."

"Like hell," Fargo said.

Lo Ping glowered and straightened and raised an arm as if to beckon to the Tong along the walls.

"That will not be necessary, Lo Ping," Han said. "What does our guest know of our customs?"

"But, great one . . . ," Lo Ping said.

Han's right eyebrow arched.

Lo Ping turned to stone. His fear was almost palpable. Quickly bowing, he said, "Your humble servant begs your forgiveness. It is unthinkable that I would question your judgment."

"Indeed," Han said. "But this one is pleased that you are so diligent in honoring our traditions."

Fargo swore he heard a sigh of relief from Lo Ping.

"Now, then," Han said, focusing on him again. "You are perhaps wondering why you were sent for."

"I've tangled with your Tong three times now," Fargo said. "I figured you'd get around to it sooner or later."

"Yes, three times," Han said. "Yet you are still alive. That is quite remarkable."

"Your boys seem to think they can push folks around," Fargo said. "Some don't take kindly to that."

"Nor would I, were the situation reversed," Han said.

"You should have a talk with Nan Kua," Fargo said. "The next time he prods me, he'll regret it."

"We will get to my unfortunate *boo how doy* in a while," Han said. "Right now I would rather talk about you." Han slowly rose and descended the dais. He moved with surprising grace, taking small steps. "Will you walk with me?"

"Where to?"

"Here is fine." Han moved past Lo Ping and began to leisurely circle the chamber. His intense eyes never once left Fargo. "Where to begin? You must have questions. Perhaps we should start with those."

"Fair enough." Fargo didn't know what to make of him. "What the hell are you up to?"

"You must be more specific."

"This gold camp. Hunan, you call it. You're making it your own little kingdom."

"Exactly so," Han said, smiling. "I could not have expressed it better myself."

"You admit it?"

"Why wouldn't I? There is, as you Americans say, no law against what I am doing, which, after all, is nothing more or less than reshaping this camp to reflect our Chinese heritage."

"Is that so?"

"Phrased more simply," Han said, "this camp will become much like Chinatown in San Francisco. Are you familiar with it?"

"Been there," Fargo said.

"Ah. Excellent. Then you can understand. It was Chinatown that gave me the idea. Walking its streets is like walking the streets of China. When we are done here, Hunan will be the same."

"I don't recollect seeing any Tong in San Francisco."

"Chinatown is much bigger than our small camp. There are, in fact, several benevolent societies in Chinatown. They compete for control."

"Benevolent?" Fargo said, and laughed.

"Scoff if you must but we are devoted to the well-being of those under us," Han said. "Under our guidance this camp will prosper as never before."

"So long as everyone does what you want."

"I can see you are a man who speaks his mind," Han said. "So I will speak mine." He stopped. "I did not come to your country willingly. There were certain difficulties, and I was forced to leave China or be thrown into prison or beheaded."

"Not much of a choice."

Han sadly frowned. "No, it was not. I miss China. To be forced to leave against my will filled me with great sorrow. But if I cannot live *in* China, I can do the next best thing. I can bring China here, as it were."

"Word is," Fargo said, "you're driving all the whites out."

"Not so," Han said. "Those who left did so of their own accord. They did not like what I am doing. And frankly, I can't blame them."

"You can't?"

"This is America, not China. Naturally, by my making this camp more reflective of our country, it made them uncomfortable."

Fargo was growing more perplexed by the minute. Based on all he'd heard, he'd taken Han for a tyrant. Instead, he was almost reasonable. "You're not at all as I reckoned you'd be," he admitted.

"I will regard that as a compliment." Han motioned and they walked on. "My dream, Mr. Fargo, is for Hunan to be a sanctuary for Chinese everywhere. Eventually, I hope it will be a city in its own right, with all the benefits that brings."

"A city in the middle of nowhere?"

"On purpose," Han said. "How do I put this delicately?" He clasped his hands behind his back. "You are aware, I should think, of the anti-Chinese sentiment in your country?"

Fargo nodded.

"Not all Americans feel that way, I know. But far too many do. They look down their noses at anyone with Chinese blood. It's all too common that Chinese are spat upon, as if they were dogs. And in some places your countrymen come in the night and drag them off and hang them from trees."

Fargo didn't say anything. Every word was true. There were even anti-Chinese leagues devoted to running the Chinese out of the country.

"Hunan will serve as a haven from all that," Han was saying while stroking his mustache. "In Hunan anyone who is Chinese need not fear for their life. In Hunan they will find only respect, and safety." Han looked at him. "Noble goals, are they not?"

"What about the House of Pleasure?"

"What about it?" Han rejoined. "It is open to all."

"I've heard tell you force girls to work in it against their will."

"Not so," Han said. "It would be most unwise. The girls would be unhappy and not perform as they should. You were there today. Did any of the female flowers you saw look unhappy to you?"

58

Fargo had to admit they didn't.

By now they were halfway around the chamber and near the double doors.

Han stopped and tapped a finger against his chin. "Have I answered most of the questions that have been bothering you?"

"Some," Fargo allowed. "But you haven't explained *them*." He nodded at the Tong.

"What is there to explain?" Han said. "They are in my employ and do the things I cannot due to my age."

"And the hatchets?"

Han grinned and nodded at the holster on Fargo's hip. "As you Americans like to say, you are a fine one to talk. Many of your countrymen go around with a firearm of one kind or another."

"Not back east," Fargo said.

"But we are not back in the East," Han replied, "and we need protection as much as you do." He nodded at the nearest Tong. "In China we do not have many guns. We have swords. And bows. And knives. And, yes, hatchets. My Tong carry them to protect themselves as you carry your revolver for protection. Surely that makes perfect sense to you?"

Again, Fargo had to admit it did.

"In time, perhaps, I will have them carry guns, as well," Han remarked. "But for now their hatchets suffice."

Fargo was tempted to point out that hatchets were no match for six-shooters, but didn't.

Suddenly Han wheeled and made for the dais. "Follow me, if you would. I have taken up too much of your time as it is and there is a matter to settle yet."

Fargo trailed after him. The meeting hadn't turned out like he thought it would. Maybe, just maybe, Han wasn't the ogre that the O'Briens and Bannon painted him as.

Climbing the dais, the old man sat in the oversized chair and adopted a regal mien. He addressed his underlings in Chinese.

"I am to tell you," Lo Ping whispered, "that my master has asked me to translate what comes next."

Han clapped his hands and a pair of Tong left the chamber. They weren't gone more than a minute. When they returned, Nan Kua was between them, his wrists bound in front of him.

"What's this?" Fargo asked.

Nan Kua was marched to the dais. He, too, bowed his head.

Han went on at some length in Chinese. Several times Nan Kua winced and once he visibly shook. Finally Han looked at Fargo. "This man is in my employ. That he attacked you without permission has brought great shame. I cannot apologize enough."

"No need," Fargo said. "It's over."

"In your eyes, perhaps. But the Tong live by a code, you might call it. When that code is broken there are consequences. I must impose those consequences or be seen as weak."

Fargo wondered what Han was leading up to. He didn't wonder long.

The venerable master of Hunan nodded at a hatchet man on Nan Kua's right. And just like that, the man buried a hatchet in Nan Kua's head.

11

It happened so fast, Fargo was caught flat-footed. Not that he would have intervened on Nan Kua's behalf.

For a few seconds Nan Kua stood still, the ax handle jutting from above his ear and blood spraying in a fine mist. Then his eyes rolled up and he collapsed. His body erupted in violent convulsions that ended with a last great exhale.

No one, not Han, not Lo Ping, or any of the Tong, so much as batted an eye. They took the death with the same detachment they would the swatting of a fly.

"Are you satisfied?" Han asked Fargo.

"You did this for me?" Fargo said.

"It was you Nan Kua and his companions tried to slay. It is only fitting you witness his punishment."

Fargo watched a pool of scarlet spread under the body.

"What about those friends of his?"

"They, too, have been punished although not as severely," Han said. "Since he was the instigator, his was the most severe."

"What did you do to them?"

"Each of them has had a hand chopped off."

Fargo stared.

"You act surprised," Han said. "They were a party to the insult. They had to atone."

"I wasn't insulted—" Fargo began, but Han cut him off with a wave of a hand.

"Oh, the insult wasn't to you. When I give orders they are to be followed. After I learned of your fight with Nan Kua and the others over the boy who took the ax, I gave

word that you were not to be interfered with in any way. By defying me, Nan Kua insulted me. And insults cannot be borne by a man in my position."

"I reckon not," Fargo said. The blood was within inches of his boots.

"I ask you again," Han said with a smile. "Are you satisfied? Have I redeemed my honor and made my sentiments clear?"

"I savvy you down to your bones," Fargo said.

"Excellent. Then there are no hard feelings between us?"

"Why would there be?"

Han appeared enormously pleased. "Our business is concluded. Lo Ping will guide you out." He waited until Fargo started to turn to add, "I should imagine you have no reason to stay in camp. A prudent man would be on his way in the morning."

"I'll keep that in mind," Fargo said.

Han smiled. "Please do so. And if your travels should ever bring you near Hunan again, you are welcome to pay us a visit."

Fargo started to turn, but stopped. He'd had a troubling thought. "What happened to the boy?"

"I beg your pardon?"

"The boy who was chopping wood. What happened to him?"

"Do you remember his name, by any chance?"

"He never told me what it was," Fargo lied.

"Ah. Well, stealing is discouraged, most strongly. When I find out who he is, he will be punished."

Fargo looked at the hatchet sticking out of the dead Tong's head. "He's just a kid."

"His age is irrelevant. It is the insult. I trust I have demonstrated they are not to be borne."

Fargo got out of there before he uttered one.

They were almost to the bottom of the stairs when Lo Ping said, "If I were you, I would take my master's advice."

"I don't aim to stick around any longer than I have to," Fargo said.

Lo Ping's cat smile widened. "You are being more reasonable than I gave you credit for."

"I can be reasonable as hell every blue moon or so."

"Blue moon? You Americans have the most peculiar expressions."

Fargo strode out. Climbing on the Ovaro, he reined in the direction of the O'Briens', and when he had gone forty or fifty feet, he stopped and looked back. Near as he could tell no one was following him.

"Reasonable, my ass," Fargo said to himself, and gigged the Ovaro to the bridge.

Every window in the House of Pleasure was lit. A pair of painted dolls stood out front, enticing passersby.

Fargo reined on up the street to an open grassy space between cabins. Halting the stallion next to a spruce, he tied the reins. He sat and removed his spurs and placed them in his saddlebags.

Loosening the Colt in its holster, Fargo glided around the cabin and on to the rear of the House of Pleasure. He was worried the door might be bolted but it creaked open. He waited in case someone had heard and when no one investigated he slipped inside and eased the door shut behind him.

A long, narrow hallway stretched ahead. From off in the distance came the murmur of conversations.

Fargo crept forward. He was moving past a flight of stairs that led down when he heard sounds from below: a harsh voice, and rattling, and what might have been a whimper. He ducked down the stairs.

There wasn't much light at first. He reached a landing, and crouched. Below was a storage area stacked with crates and containers, nearly all with Chinese writing or symbols on them. An aisle had been cleared through the center, and from behind a high wall of crates rosy light filtered in.

A man barked in Chinese. A woman mewled as if in pain. Chains rattled, and there was the unmistakable sharp crack of a slap.

Palming his Colt, Fargo continued down. He peeked up the aisle. All he could see was a Tong with his back to him.

There were more barking and more blows.

Fargo moved on silent soles. He was about ten feet from the Tong when he came to another aisle at a right angle to the first. It ran along the wall of crates. He moved along it until he spied a gap between two of the crates.

One look, and his blood boiled.

Three young Chinese women were bound to chairs; one was Mai Wing. They had been stripped to the waist and their bodies bore scores of bruises and contusions. Their faces, though, hadn't been touched. Each sat slumped with exhaustion, their heads hung low.

As Fargo watched, another Tong came into view and cupped Mai Wing's chin. He raised her head and grinned and said something.

Mai Wing spat on him.

The Tong punched her in the gut and she sagged, gasping.

A third Tong, out of sight to Fargo's left, voiced a comment that brought a chuckle to the hatchet man who had hit her.

Fargo debated. Shots were bound to bring more men in black. The quieter, the better, then. Sliding the Colt into his holster, he hiked his pant leg, dipped his hand into his boot, and slid the Arkansas toothpick from its ankle sheath.

Retracing his steps to the main aisle, Fargo peered around. The first Tong still stood there with his back to him. He heard the other two talking.

Quickly, with no wasted motion, Fargo reached around and clamped his left hand over the man's mouth even as he thrust the toothpick in to the hilt into the side of man's neck. The Tong stiffened and clutched at his arm but was dead within heartbeats.

Catching the heavy body as it fell, Fargo dragged it behind the crates and quietly placed it on the floor. He moved to where the man had been standing and craned his head out.

The other two Tong were facing the three young women.

The same one who had cupped Mai Wing's chin before cupped it again. This time she didn't spit on him. Her eyes were dazed, almost glassy. From her bruises, they had been hurting her a good long while.

Fargo crept to a point directly behind her tormentors.

They were enjoying themselves, these two. The one on the left was slightly behind the other, and Fargo took him first. In a long bound he reached him and did as he had done with the first: hand over the mouth, cold steel in the neck. Fargo knew exactly where to stab so that death was near instantaneous. He didn't bother trying to catch this one as the body collapsed. He sprang at the other, seeking to dispose of him just as quickly.

The last man spun. He snarled in Chinese and suddenly an ax was in his hand. He sidestepped Fargo's thrust and swung his ax at Fargo's head.

Fargo caught his wrist. The Tong caught his. Locked together, they struggled. Fargo was strong but so was the Tong. Fargo used his advantage in height to slowly bend the Tong back. The man did more snarling. Without warning, he drove a knee at Fargo's groin and wrenched to break free.

Fargo let go, and drove his boot at the Tong's knee.

The man cried out and staggered. Fargo slashed him across the wrist but the Tong held on to the hatchet and aimed a blow at Fargo's neck. Dodging, Fargo cut him across the other leg. The man tottered and retaliated. Fargo ducked, shifted, and rammed the toothpick into the Tong's jugular. He grabbed the man's wrist and held it as life ebbed. Defiant to the last, the Tong tried to gouge out his eyes. Then he went limp.

Fargo let him drop. He wiped the toothpick clean of blood on the dead man's shirt and moved to Mai Wing.

"You," she croaked in some amazement.

"Can you walk?" Fargo asked as he cut at the ropes with short, swift strokes.

"You came to find me?"

"I'm here," Fargo said, listening for sounds from above. More Tong might show at any moment.

"You hardly know me."

"I can go and leave you tied to the chair if you want," Fargo said. He sliced through the last loop and put an arm around her shoulders. "Can you stand?"

"I think so." Wincing, Mai Wing stiffly rose. The first thing she did was bend and pick up her top, which had been shoved under her chair.

"How long have they been working on you?"

"After you were struck down, Lo Ping and the Hu brothers took me to Han and then here," Mai Wing related as she painfully slipped an arm into a sleeve. "The Pou sisters were already being tortured. They, too, do not want to be whores."

"Lean on the chair," Fargo directed. She was terribly weak. He made short shrift of the ropes on the other two and helped them to stand. They were weaker and had more contusions and black and blue marks.

Mai Wing helped them put their tops on.

"I've got to get you out of here," Fargo said when she was done. "Are the three of you up to it?"

"I am," Mai Wing said. She addressed the Pou sisters, and after a brief exchange, she frowned. "They have not had food or water for three days. They do not know if they can."

"They have to try," Fargo said. "I can't help them and protect you at the same time."

Mai Wing said more to the sisters and both responded with what sounded to Fargo like *she* or *shi*. "They say they will try their best."

"Stay behind me." Fargo drew his Colt. With the six-shooter in one hand and the toothpick in the other, he led them to the foot of the stairs.

Mai Wing could move fairly well but the other two were turtles. One wobbled every few steps and her sister had to steady her.

Fargo frowned. It was a long way up. "Is there another way out?"

"There is the ramp. It is how they bring things in." Mai Wing motioned at the front wall.

"Show me."

They turned and had no sooner taken a couple of steps than voices wafted down from the top of the stairs.

12

Fargo raised the Colt but Mai Wing put her hand on his arm.

"No," she whispered. "They are on their way out the back."

Sure enough, the voices faded.

The ramp was about six feet wide. Double doors were fitted with large rollers at street level.

Fargo took hold of a handle and tugged. The door slid easily enough, and he cracked it open a few inches. He could see the stream, and across it, Han's towering Pagoda. He could also see several Tong loitering near the bridge. If he opened the door all the way, they were bound to spot him. "We'll wait a few minutes."

Mai Wing put her hands on her knees and bent over and groaned.

"How bad?" Fargo asked.

"I am dizzy," Mai Wing said. "They hit me on the head."

"But not in the face."

"No," Mai Wing said bitterly. "So we could go to work for Madame Lotus that much sooner. The face is very important."

Fargo recollected the painted faces of the women in the parlor. "They took it for granted you'd give in."

"They bragged that everyone does, sooner or later. There is only so much pain a person can take."

One of the Pou sisters fell to her knees and the other sister comforted her. They whispered, and one spoke to Mai Wing.

"She says that her sister is badly hurt inside. One of the Tong kicked her. She does not know if she can go on."

"She has to try," Fargo said. He peered out again. The Tong by the bridge were drifting up the street. The moment they were out of sight he opened the door wide enough for them to slip through. He helped Mai Wing and then the Pous.

Off to the left was the entrance to the House of Pleasure. Two painted girls were leaning against the wall and hadn't noticed them. Nor did anyone passing by pay any attention.

Minding one's business might as well have been a law in Hunan.

"Where can I take you?" Fargo wondered if the O'Briens might help. Then again, it might put the family in danger.

"My grandfather," Mai Wing said, and pointed to the east. "If we can reach his cabin. But there are always Tong out and around."

"I have an idea," Fargo said, and ushered them around the corner. "Stay put. I'll be right back."

Fargo practically ran to the Ovaro. Swinging onto the saddle, he rode back up the street. The two girls glanced at him and went on talking. He went around to the side and drew rein. "Give me directions as we go. I'll go slow."

"The Tong will see you," Mai Wing said. "On your animal you are conspicuous."

"But they won't see you on the other side," Fargo hoped. It wasn't much of a plan but it was the best he could come up with.

With the Ovaro moving at a walk and the sisters leaning on the stallion to keep from falling, they covered the quarter mile or so to a short side street. Along the way Fargo spotted half a dozen Tong. Apparently word had gone out from Han not to give him any trouble, which worked in their favor.

"This is the one," Mai Wing said as they neared the last cabin on the right.

The windows were dark. She had to knock for a good two minutes before a light flared and shuffling steps came from the other side of the door. A man evidently asked who it was, and she answered.

Fargo rode around to the side so the Ovaro was out of sight, and dismounted. He reached the door just as an old

man in a nightshirt was about to close it. His presence seemed to startle the oldster and he drew back in alarm.

Mai Wing calmed him. The old man helped her—reluctantly, Fargo thought—seat the Pou sisters, and commenced to put tea on.

Fargo shut the door and leaned against it. "You can't stay here long," he said to Mai Wing. "The Tong must know he's your kin."

"They do," Mai Wing confirmed. "But we should have time to eat and drink and tend our wounds. After that, I do not know."

Fargo thought of the O'Briens again. "I know some people who might be willing to help. It shouldn't take me more than twenty minutes to get there and back." He didn't like the idea of leaving her. Once the bodies in the House of Pleasure were discovered, the Tong would be after them like bloodhounds on a scent.

"You have already done so much. I cannot ask you to do more."

"Who said you had to ask?"

"If the Tong find us, they will kill you for helping us escape."

"What's your point?"

"Please. Do not make light of this. I would not have your life on my conscience."

"Twenty minutes," Fargo said, and went back out. He saw no sign of the Tong until he was almost to the bridge, and once again they showed no interest in him. Crossing over, he was passing the blacksmith shop when a brainstorm struck like a thunderclap. "Why didn't I think of it sooner?" he said to the Ovaro, and reined over.

Fargo knocked but there was no answer. He tried the latch. The door was bolted. Walking around to the side, he looked in a window. A lit lantern hung from a peg, casting enough light to show that no one was there.

A noise drew Fargo to the rear.

A horse had been hitched to a buckboard and Tom Bannon was loading tools and personal effects into the bed. He had on his leather apron.

"Bannon," Fargo said by way of greeting.

The blacksmith whirled and grabbed for a hammer. "You!" he blurted, and relaxed and smiled.

Fargo nodded at the buckboard. "Are you still fixing to leave?"

"Need you ask?" Bannon rejoined. "I can't take any more of this place. I'm getting out in the middle of the night, as planned."

"Is there room for three more?"

"What are you talking about?"

Quickly, Fargo explained about Mai Wing and the Pou sisters.

Bannon swore luridly, then said, "It doesn't surprise me a bit, Han forcing girls to sell their bodies."

"Does that mean you will or you won't?" Fargo was eager to get back.

"There's not a lot of room left," Bannon said. "But I suppose if one of them rides on the seat with me and the other two are willing to sit in the back, we can manage."

"I'll go give them the news."

"One thing," Bannon said as Fargo turned. "I don't mind taking them so long as they don't mind going east. I'm heading for Denver. They can ride with me the whole distance or I'll let them off anywhere they want along the way."

"What time are you leaving?"

Bannon took a pocket watch from his apron and opened it. "Let's say two o'clock. Have them here by one thirty."

"They'll be here."

Fargo didn't spot any Tong on his way back to the cabin. He knocked, and Mai Wing opened the door to admit him. She had cleaned herself up and combed her hair.

The Pou sisters were huddled by the fireplace. The one who had been kicked was leaning against the other, and pasty with sweat.

Fargo went to tell Mai Wing about the blacksmith, and realized someone was missing. "Where's your grandpa?"

"He went to a healer for herbs," Mai Wing revealed. "He should return soon."

Fargo told her about Bannon and his buckboard, ending

with, "You can say adios to this place forever. I'll help you gather up whatever you'd like to take."

"Whatever made you think I would leave?"

For a moment Fargo was dumbfounded. "How in hell can you stay after what the Tong did to you?"

"My grandfather is here. My friends are here." Mai Wing shook her head. "I cannot go."

Fargo couldn't believe what he was hearing. "You ran away earlier."

"They were chasing me. I would have snuck back later if they hadn't seen the smoke from your fire and caught me."

"You're not safe here, damn it."

"I am sorry."

Fargo gestured at the sisters. "What about those two? Do they want to stay too?"

Mai Wing put the question to the siblings. "They say they will accept your gracious offer," she translated their response.

"They have more sense than you do."

"If you were in my shoes I doubt you would run," Mai Wing countered. "Why do you hold it against me for doing what you would do?"

Fargo had no answer for that. He leaned against the wall while she poured tea for the sisters. He admired her grit, but if Han got his hands on her again, there was no telling what the little monster would do.

Someone rapped on the door.

Fargo placed his hand on his Colt.

Mai Wing brushed past, saying, "There is no need for that. It will be my grandfather."

She was right. The old man entered and chattered at the women.

Mai Wing looked crestfallen. "He says the healer wasn't in," she reported. "He'll have to go back in a while to see about the herbs."

"It might be best to forget about them," Fargo cautioned.

"No. You can see how poorly the younger Pou is doing. Without them she might die."

"If it's not chickens, it's feathers."

72

"Sorry?"

"Nothing," Fargo said grumpily. He could have done with some coffee. He asked if there was any to be had and she relayed that her grandfather only drank tea. "Figures," he muttered.

The old man, Fargo noticed, was wringing his hands and acting as nervous as a canary in a room full of cats. He attributed it to harboring the women.

Then the Ovaro whinnied.

Fargo darted to the window and warily peered out without showing himself.

Dark figures were closing on the cabin. The Tong had found them.

13

Even as Fargo set eyes on them, a tremendous crash shook the front door and a pair of brawny hatchet men spilled into the room.

One of the Pou sisters screamed.

The foremost Tong saw Mai Wing and moved toward her, raising his hatchet.

Fargo shot him in the head.

The second Tong glanced over and rushed him, letting out a cry of rage.

Fargo shot him in the chest. At his elbow the window shattered in an explosion of glass shards and a thrown hatchet arced past his face. Pivoting, he beheld two Tong just outside. He shot them both.

Mai Wing yelled a warning.

Yet another Tong was coming through the front door. He whipped his arm back to throw his hatchet.

"Drop it," Fargo warned, extending his Colt.

The man hesitated.

"You don't have to die," Fargo said.

Mai Wing said something, apparently translating.

The Tong glanced at her and then at Fargo. He started to lower his hatchet, or pretended to. With a shout, he suddenly straightened and his arm arced.

Fargo shot him before the hatchet left his hand.

Grabbing at his face, the Tong took a faltering step and folded.

In the silence that ensued, Fargo's ears rang. Mai Wing stared at the dead Tong. The Pou sisters were crouched in fear.

Over in a corner, the grandfather gaped aghast at the slaughter.

Fargo went to the door. They didn't have a lot of time. The gunshots would bring more. He hastily reloaded, snapping over his shoulder, "We have to leave. Now."

"I told you I'm not going," Mai Wing said.

"You stay and they'll kill you," Fargo predicted. He motioned at the bodies. "Han won't let you live after this."

"They must have followed us without us knowing," Mai Wing said.

"No," Fargo said. "Your grandfather brought them."

"That cannot be," Mai Wing said, and turned to the old man. The look on his face said all there was to say.

"Grandfather?" she said in English, and switched to Chinese.

Fargo went out and around to the Ovaro. He figured if he could get them to one of the pockets of woodland that dotted the canyon floor, they'd lie low for a couple of hours and he'd take them to the blacksmith's after things quieted down.

Mai Wing was in tears. She came to him and placed her hands on his chest. "You were right. He told them where I was." She sobbed, and caught herself. "He betrayed my trust for money."

Fargo remembered a comment Lo Ping made when they first met. "Five will get you ten he's the one who sold you to Madame Lotus."

Shock set Mai Wing back on her heels. She looked at her grandfather and more tears flowed. "How could he do this to me?" she said, to herself more than to Fargo.

"We have to go."

Mai Wing blinked and dabbed at her eyes. "I am sorry. Yes. More of them will come." She went to the sisters and helped them to stand. As they came toward the door, her grandfather barred their way.

The grandfather pointed at Mai Wing and said something and she looked at Fargo.

"He says that if I were a dutiful granddaughter, I would let the Tong take me to the House of Pleasure."

"Tell him to get the hell out of your way."

"He says he won't."

"Fine," Fargo said, and drawing his Colt, he slammed it against the old man's head. Not anywhere near hard enough to kill but hard enough that the old man sprawled unconscious.

Mai Wing stifled a sob. "I love him so much. He was all the family I had left in the world."

They hurried out.

Fargo had her explain to the Pou sisters what he was about to do, then swung each up and over the saddle. With the sisters clinging to each other and Mai Wing at his side, he headed west along the canyon wall until they came to a stand of trees.

"This should do us for a spell."

Fargo helped the sisters off. He untied his bedroll, spread out his blankets, and through Mai Wing, told them they were welcome to lie down and rest. They gladly accepted.

Shucking the Henry from the saddle scabbard, Fargo moved to where he could see their back trail. He doubted the Tong would attempt to track them at night, but better safe than dead. Hunkering, he set the rifle across his lap and wearily rubbed his eyes.

Soft footfalls heralded Mai Wing. She eased down next to him and whispered, "They are asleep already."

"You should try to get some rest yourself."

"I'm too upset over my grandfather. The pain doesn't help, either." She bent nearer. "There is something I would like to know."

Fargo was straining to hear sounds from the vicinity of the cabin.

"Why did you come for me? And this time give me an honest answer, if you please."

"One of the Hu brothers hit me over the head and left me lying in the dirt."

"What does that have to do with me?"

"The Hus work for Han."

"I still don't understand. Unless you are saying that by

saving me, you get back at him for the indignity of being laid low."

"That's as good a reason as any," Fargo said.

"All this is to you is revenge? I do not believe it for a minute."

Fargo shrugged. "Suit yourself."

Mia Wing put her hand on his knee. "Thank you. I am in your debt. Whatever you ask of me, I will do."

"Remind me of that after you've healed up," Fargo said with a grin.

An occasional voice and once the sound of laughter drifted to them from Hunan. Then there were shouts, and lights bobbed up and down the main street and along the side streets.

"The Tong are searching for us." Mai Wing stated the obvious.

"We're safe enough here."

"They will not rest until they find us."

Fargo grunted.

"Han will want your head. He can't let you live after you have killed so many of his hatchet men. The rest would resent it."

"I aim to deal with him, too." Fargo sensed she was studying him in the dark. "Don't make more of it than there is."

"You are one against many."

"Chop off a snake's head and the snake dies."

"Should you succeed in slaying Han, Lo Ping will assume his place."

"Two heads, then."

"I wish I had your confidence. I have never been very strong."

"You stood up to Han."

"Only because I refuse to let men I do not know run their hands over me. It is *my* body. I should have a say, don't you think?"

"No one should touch you if you don't want them to," Fargo agreed.

"Isn't that in your— What do you call the document? Your Constitution?"

"I don't know as there is anything in there about touching."

"You haven't read it?" Mai Wing asked in surprise.

"I had a little schooling when I was a kid and the teacher talked about it some. But, no, I've never read the thing. What I remember most is that I have the right to wear this." Fargo patted the Colt. "And any son of a bitch who says I can't will eat his teeth."

"Maybe I am mistaken," Mai Wing said. "Maybe the touching is in your Bible. The Ten Commandments, I believe they are called. Do you know them?"

"I recollect my pa going on about honor thy father and thy mother," Fargo quoted. "And there's another one that we're not supposed to kill."

"Yet you do."

"When an Apache comes at me with a knife in his hand or one of those Tong with his hatchet, you're damn right I do."

"So you are not what Americans would call religious?"

Fargo thought of all the women he'd made love to and all the whiskey he'd sucked down and the countless hours he'd spent playing poker and the enemies he had bucked out in gore. "Most folks would say I'm anything but." He paused. "Why the hell are we talking about this?"

"I am sorry if I have upset you," Mai Wing said contritely. "I just want someone to talk to. So I do not think of . . . what has happened."

"Flap your gums all you want then," Fargo said, feeling guilty.

"Do you think your God is mad at you for killing?"

Fargo looked at her. "You ask the strangest damn questions. How would I know what God thinks?"

"My people do not believe as your people do. But if there is a God, I find it strange that God said we should not kill when God kills. We are born but to die—is that not so?"

"Damn it, woman," Fargo said. "My head is about to explode."

"Again, I am sorry. You do not like to talk about these things, do you?"

"Not if I can help it."

In the quiet that followed they could hear yells and saw dozens of lanterns flitting about like oversized fireflies.

"They will go through the entire camp from end to end."

"Likely so."

"Would you mind if I used you as a pillow?" Mai Wing asked.

Before Fargo could answer, she shifted and lowered her head to his leg and placed her cheek on his thigh.

"Is this all right?"

"Fine," Fargo growled. It was a shame, he reflected, that they couldn't make love. "I'll wake you when it's time."

"Should the Tong kill you, I will burn incense in your honor and remember you until the day I die."

Fargo supposed she meant that as a compliment of some sort. "Get some sleep."

Mai Wing was still a bit, and then said softly, "Before this is over, there will be a lot more killing, won't there?"

"A hell of a lot," Fargo said.

14

The passage of the Big Dipper and the North Star through the heavens was as reliable as the hour hand of a pocket watch.

It was about one in the morning when Fargo shook Mai Wing's shoulder. She awoke with a start and sat up and blurted something in Chinese.

"Calm down," Fargo said. "You're not in the House of Pleasure, remember?"

Mai Wing looked around in confusion. "Oh," she said. "For a moment there—" She smoothed her hair and her top. "I apologize."

"For what?" Fargo said. "After what you went through, it's natural."

"Is it time?" she asked.

"Almost." Fargo had to have them at the blacksmith's by one thirty. He rose and helped Mai Wing stand.

The Pou sisters were sound asleep, each with a cheek on the arm of the other.

Fargo let Mai Wing wake them. They were slow to rouse, and the younger was still in great pain. While they collected themselves, he rolled up his blankets and tied his bedroll on the Ovaro.

The night was practically silent. The shouting in Hunan had died down and fireflies no longer flitted here and there.

Fargo gave the sisters a boost onto the saddle. The younger could barely walk and the other was so weak, she would tire in no time. Mai Wing wasn't much better off but she was tougher and insisted she could keep up.

They traveled along the canyon wall until in Fargo's estimation they were abreast of the stable.

A side street brought them to the main one, and a bridge that would take them across the stream.

Not a soul was abroad. Nearly all the buildings were dark.

That included the blacksmith's.

Fargo tried the front door but it wouldn't open. He went around to the side, Mai Wing at his elbow, the Ovaro's hooves clomping dully.

The buckboard was still there, a space in the bed clear for the sisters. The horse was dozing.

Fargo went to the back door. It was open a crack. He pushed and entered and whispered Bannon's name several times.

There was no reply.

Puzzled, Fargo went back out. "I reckon he'll be along any minute," he told Mai Wing. He helped the sisters down and they sat next to the wagon with their arms around each other.

Minute after minute crawled by until they had been waiting half an hour.

"Where can he be?" Mai Wing whispered.

Fargo had no idea. He noticed one of the sisters shiver even though it wasn't all that chilly and suggested they go into the shop to wait. "We'll be out of the wind."

Bannon's living quarters were to one side. The room was crammed and untidy but there was an old couch the sisters gratefully collapsed on.

Fargo was tempted to light a lamp but didn't. It would have given them away. He moved to the front door, threw the bolt, and opened it a hair. He wasn't surprised when an arm brushed his.

"Am I right in thinking something is wrong?" Mai Wing asked.

"Maybe he changed his mind with all the ruckus," Fargo mused. It could be that Bannon had decided to delay leaving for a day or two.

"But why is he not here? Where would he go at this hour?"

A notion came to Fargo. "I have an idea. Keep watch over those other two for a while. I won't be long."

"Where are you going?" Mai Wing anxiously asked.

"The O'Briens'." Fargo figured that was the logical place to look. Bannon and the family were friends. He slipped out and worked his way to their house without once seeing a living soul. Hunan might as well have been a ghost town.

The O'Brien house was as dark as every other.

Fargo climbed the steps and knocked. Not too loudly, so the neighbors wouldn't hear. No one came so he knocked again. Once more, nothing.

Stepping back, Fargo cast about for small stones. He found a few and stood under a second-floor window and threw one. It struck the glass with a *clack*. He had to throw three more before the curtain moved and a silhouette appeared. There was the rasp of the window being raised, and Terrence O'Brien poked his head out.

"Fargo? Is that you, boyo? What in God's name are you doing here at this ungodly hour?"

"Looking for Tom Bannon," Fargo whispered up.

"Why would he be here?"

"He's not at his shop. I didn't know where else he might be."

"Hold on. I'm coming down."

Fargo waited at the door. It wasn't long before the bolt rasped and it was jerked open.

O'Brien had donned a bulky robe and slippers. He stepped out and closed the door after him. "I don't want to wake Noirin. She's been having bad nights of late and can use the sleep. Now what's this about Tom?"

Fargo explained about the women waiting at Bannon's.

"Dear God. Then that commotion was about you? We saw Tong going door to door but they never came to ours."

"Strange," Fargo said. He would have thought that their place was one of the first Han would look.

"As for Tom, the last I saw him, he was dead set on leaving tonight."

"I'd best get back," Fargo said.

"Listen. If Tom doesn't show, you and the ladies are welcome to stay at our house for the rest of the night."

"I'm obliged." As Fargo turned he thought he spied movement a few houses away. He stopped and peered intently but saw no one.

The walk back seemed to take forever. A sense of unease crept over him, like the time he was being stalked by a Sioux war party, and more recently when he was being hunted on the plains of Texas by a man with a Sharps.

He saw no one, heard no one.

The blacksmith's shop was quiet but it should have been. The women wouldn't want to draw attention. He opened the door and went in and said, "Mai Wing? Where are you?"

"I am here, Skye," she answered from the back.

Something in her voice wasn't right. His hand on his Colt, Fargo moved toward Bannon's living quarters. He was halfway there when a lucifer was struck and applied to the wick of a lantern.

Lo Ping was holding it. "Before you do anything rash, American," he said in his oily manner, "consider the consequences." He held the lantern higher.

One of the Hu brothers had hold of Mai Wing's hair, his hatchet to her throat. All it would take was a swipe of his hand and she was as good as dead.

Near them, on their knees, were the Pou sisters. The other Hu was behind them, his hatchet raised to strike.

"That is not all," Lo Ping said, and gestured.

More lanterns blazed, revealing twenty or more Tong. Two were armed with rifles, pointed at Fargo's chest.

"You are quick enough that you would kill some of us," Lo Ping said, "but you would assuredly die, and the women, as well."

Fargo fumed at his blunder in walking right into their little trap.

"Nothing to say?" Lo Ping taunted.

"Go to hell."

"I am Chinese. I do not believe in what you would call fairy tales." Lo Ping smiled. "In case you are wondering

how we knew to find you here, you have the blacksmith to thank."

"Bannon told you I was bringing them?"

"Reluctantly. You see, after you shot so many of our Tong brothers, we left no stone unturned in trying to find you." Lo Ping came closer. "We discovered Mr. Bannon loading his buckboard. My master ordered that he be brought to the Pagoda and after some . . . persuasion . . . he told us how you had stopped by and asked him if he would take the women."

"You tortured him."

"Not I personally," Lo Ping said. "I am, I am sorry to admit, squeamish about blood. The Hu brothers were the ones who loosened his tongue."

"What now?" Fargo demanded.

"I should think it would be obvious," Lo Ping rejoined. "You will unbuckle your gun belt and set it on the floor. Then you will raise your arms in the air and we will take you to Master Han."

Fargo glanced at Mai Wing, and hesitated.

"Come now," Lo Ping said. "It is not as if you have a choice. Give us trouble and the women die. Do as we say and you, and they, go on breathing."

"For how long?"

Lo Ping shrugged. "That is for my master to say. He is the one you have wronged. He is the one you must answer to."

Fargo dearly wanted to put a slug through the smug snake's brainpan. Instead, using two fingers, he removed his gun belt and placed it at his feet.

"There," Lo Ping gloated. "That wasn't so hard, was it?"

"Bastard," Fargo said.

"You are most indiscreet in your comments," Lo Ping criticized. "How you have lived as long as you have is a mystery."

A Tong cautiously came over and snatched the gun belt off the floor.

"Let Mai Wing go," Fargo said to the Hu holding her.

"I am afraid he doesn't speak your barbaric tongue," Lo Ping said. Reverting to Chinese, he must have translated

because the Hu glared and said something that made a lot of the other Tong smile. "He says that he doesn't take orders from a white cur."

"What harm can it do?"

Lo Ping didn't bother to translate. "She is our insurance that you will not try anything. The sisters, too. But I suspect Mai Wing means more to you."

"We are friends, nothing more," Mai Wing said, and the Hu brother holding her shook her savagely.

"Not another word out of you, woman," Lo Ping said. "You have not only disgraced your grandfather—you have insulted Master Han. While the first is perhaps forgivable, the second is not."

Mai Wing wasn't intimidated. "He intends to kill us, doesn't he?" she asked in English.

"It is not for me to pretend to know the thoughts of the inscrutable one," Lo Ping said. "But if I were you, I would make peace with myself."

"What about me?" Fargo said.

"For you, American, there will be no peace. For you, very soon, there will only be oblivion."

15

Han sat on his throne with the regal air of an emperor. Or as Fargo liked to think of him, a shrunken praying mantis. His thin fingers a tepee in his lap, the lord of Hunan smiled a benign smile as Fargo and the women were shoved and manhandled to the dais.

The Pou sisters fell to their knees and broke into sobs.

Han said a few words in Chinese and wagged a finger, and they covered their mouths with their hands and the sobs subsided.

"As you commanded, great one," Lo Ping said in English, evidently for Fargo's benefit. "Here are the buckskin and the runaway."

"The scout can wait," Han said, and focused on Mai Wing. "What do you have to say for yourself, young woman?"

She glared in defiance.

"You are a disgrace to your family," Han intoned. "Your grandfather placed you in my care and you rebuff my kindness at every turn."

"Care!" Mai Wing exploded. "Kindness? You intend for me to work in the House of Pleasure."

"What other use is there for a female your age?" Han said. "I could have put you to scrubbing floors or cooking. Tiresome, monotonous work. But I did not. I offered you an easier position with Madame Lotus, and all you have done is give her trouble."

"I refuse to sell my body," Mai Wing said.

"You are not selling it for you," Han said. "You are selling it for me."

"As if that makes a difference. You don't have the right to make me. We're in America now, not China."

"Dear child." Han chuckled. "While we might be *in* America, we are not part *of* America. Here the old ways apply. Here you are in China, and Chinese ways are the only ways."

"Like hell," Fargo broke in.

Lo Ping nodded at one of the Hus.

Fargo tried to turn but he wasn't fast enough. A blow to his kidney almost made him cry out. As it was, he pitched onto his left knee and doubled over in agony.

"You will address Master Han only when spoken to," Lo Ping said. "And you will address him with the respect he deserves."

"I did," Fargo puffed between gasps for breath.

Lo Ping nodded again but Han held up a hand.

"No more of that, for now." Han smiled. "These Americans do so love to bluster, do they not?"

"Exactly so, great one," Lo Ping said.

Fargo was thinking that this made twice he owed the Hu brothers. Both times the bastards had struck him from behind.

"Take the scout below and put him with the other one," Master Han commanded. "The girl goes back to Madame Lotus. And this time make sure she stays there."

Lo Ping did another of his subservient bows. "Your will be done."

Fargo still hurt like hell. That didn't stop him from suddenly rising and lunging at the throne, his fist bunched to smash the mighty Han in the face. Quick as he was, though, the Hus were quicker. Iron hands clamped on each wrist and he was slammed onto his back on the floor. Metal glinted before his eyes. Another hatchet was pressed to his neck.

Han spat in Chinese, then switched to English again. "Will you never learn? Do you have any idea how close you came?"

"You better do it now, you son of a bitch," Fargo growled.

"And deprive myself of the pleasure of crushing your

spirit before I destroy your body and mind?" Han said. "I think not."

"Great one," Lo Ping said. "You can see how he is. Permit me to have him hamstrung so he does not give us as much trouble."

"Have we become weaklings?" Han countered. "Or are we stronger and more intelligent and more patient than he and his kind?"

"We are, O celestial one."

"You will do as I say. I want him in full vigor when I break him. It will make his humiliation that much worse for him to bear."

"As always, you think far ahead of me," Lo Ping said.

"It is why I am sitting here," Han said, "and you are standing there." He waved a hand. "Off with him. Then have the sisters taken to my private chambers and strip them and have them wash. I will be there later to let them entertain me."

"Consider it done," Lo Ping said. He issued orders to the men in black.

Mai Wing shot Fargo a look of despair as he was seized by half a dozen hatchet men and dragged to a side passage. They held him so firmly, to resist would have been futile.

Lo Ping led the way down a narrow flight of stairs into the bowels of the Pagoda. Here and there in nooks in the walls were small flickering lamps that cast writhing shadows.

At the bottom was a circular room with heavy doors spaced about ten feet apart. Each had a barred window. The occupants had heard them coming and haggard faces peered out.

"A dungeon?" Fargo said in disbelief.

"We have many in China," Lo Ping said. "Another of our traditions you Americans could benefit from." Producing a large key ring, he selected a key. "I only hope my master permits me to witness your degradation. There are few things I enjoy more than to hear someone scream. It is music to the ears."

"I'll remember that when your time comes."

Lo Ping sighed. "Too much bluster is childish." He inserted the key and twisted it and pulled.

Fargo tried to drag his heels but the Tong effortlessly shoved him in and the door slammed shut behind him. He found himself in a stone-walled chamber with only a candle for light.

Lo Ping's face appeared at the bars. "You and your friend can discuss your mutual stupidity in the time you have left." He showed his teeth, and was gone.

"My friend?" Fargo said to the walls.

"That would be me," Tom Bannon said, and shuffled out of a dark corner. He was a mess. His clothes were torn. His face was black and blue and spattered with dried blood and one eye was swollen.

"Hell," Fargo said.

"I have you to thank for this," Bannon said. "I hear you shot a bunch of Tong. They went over every square foot of this camp looking for you and found me loading my wagon."

"So I heard."

"I don't hold it against you," the blacksmith declared. "You did what you had to. Did the women get away?"

"Han has them."

"Hell." Bannon stepped to a wall and turned and sat with his back to it. "I reckon we're in for it come morning."

"I thought Han needed you," Fargo said.

"I'm the only blacksmith for two hundred miles," Bannon said. "But I was trying to run out on him and he's not the forgiving sort."

Fargo grunted. Neither was he. He moved to the opposite wall and wearily sank down.

"What about the O'Briens?" Bannon asked.

"Fine, as far as I know." Fargo hoped they stayed that way. He had enough on his hands at the moment.

"He'll carve on us, you know," Bannon said. "Or his butcher boys will. While he watches and gloats."

Fargo touched his empty holster. They'd taken his Colt but he still had an ace down his boot.

The blacksmith was in a talkative mood. "I heard a

word once," he said. "Sadist. Never paid it much mind. But I have since Han took over. He's a sadistic bastard. I wouldn't put it past him to have us chopped to bits and then dance on the pieces."

"I hope he slips and breaks his scrawny neck."

Tom Bannon laughed. "I like you, mister. You never give up or give in."

"Do you think they'll bring us breakfast?"

"How can you think of food at a time like this?"

Fargo was thinking of the Arkansas toothpick.

"They might, though," Bannon said. "Han will want us hearty and hale when the knives start on us. More fun for him that way."

"I'd like to slit his scrawny throat," Fargo mentioned.

"Stand in line. I was here first." Bannon sagged, and yawned. "I was up all day, and then all that loading. I don't mind admitting I'm plumb tuckered out. I need some sleep."

"Good idea," Fargo said. He'd need his wits about him come the dawn. Settling back, he pulled his hat brim over his face.

"All that counts now," Tom Bannon remarked, "is that one of us lives long enough to do Han in."

Of that, Fargo vowed, he'd make certain. He closed his eyes and within moments drifted into a nightmare where he was pursued by shapeless demons dressed in black. He woke in a cold sweat.

The candle had burned down to a nub.

Even without a window he knew it was close to dawn. For years his habit was to awaken at the break of day.

Fargo got up and paced. It took him past the door, and each time he looked through the bars. A lot depended on them bringing breakfast. First and foremost, his life.

Bannon had been snoring but now he sputtered and sat up and opened his eyes. "You're up already?"

"What I wouldn't give for coffee," Fargo said.

Bannon scratched and rubbed the stubble on his chin. "You and me, both. I wish to hell—"

"Wait," Fargo said, holding up a hand for quiet. There had been a faint sound. Putting his ear to the bars, he caught

more: the scrape of sandals on the stairs. "Someone is coming."

"It could be they're just checking on us."

Bending, Fargo pulled up his pant leg and palmed the toothpick.

"Well, now," the blacksmith said. "Aren't you a bundle of tricks?" Bracing himself, he rose. "Any help I can be, say the word."

"Let's see how many we're up against."

Two Tong. One carried a tray with bread and water. They came straight to Fargo's cell and the other one spat Chinese and motioned for him to step back.

Fargo was all too happy to comply. But only a couple of steps. He held the toothpick close against his leg where it couldn't be seen.

A key scraped in the lock and the door began to swing open.

16

Fargo wasn't holding back any longer. The pair who entered was as good as dead and didn't know it.

The one with a hatchet motioned for him to move farther away, and he did. Then the Tong with the tray moved to one side to set it down.

The Tong with the hatchet glanced at Tong setting the tray down.

It was all the opening Fargo needed. He sprang and rammed the Arkansas toothpick up under the man's sternum, piercing the heart. The Tong opened his mouth to cry out but died before he could utter a sound.

Wrenching the toothpick out, Fargo charged the tray bearer. The man was unfurling. His eyes registered shock in the instant before Fargo slit his throat from ear to ear.

Fargo stepped back to avoid the scarlet spray. It was over surprisingly fast, after some gurgling and thrashing.

"God in heaven," Tom Bannon breathed.

Fargo wiped the toothpick on the man's clothes, slid it into its sheath, and helped himself to a hatchet. Different from those sold in America, it was lighter and the handle curved slightly. The edge was sharp as a razor. "Grab the other one."

Bannon nodded and bent. "What next?"

Fargo found the keys. He went out and over to the next cell and had to try three keys before he found the right one.

The prisoner who emerged was a walking skeleton, his clothes so many rags. He was missing an ear and several fingers and had deep cuts on his face and neck. He was also white.

"Good God!" Bannon blurted. "I know this man."

"Hello, Tom," the apparition rasped.

"This is Chester Arnold," Bannon introduced him. "He had a claim on the creek. One of the biggest and best. One day the word went through camp that he'd been off chopping firewood and been attacked and killed by a grizzly."

"Han's doing," Arnold said, and his eyes blazed with hate.

"You'll help us?" Fargo asked.

"If it involves killing Han, I sure as hell will," Arnold declared.

Fargo moved to the next cell. He didn't know how long it would be before the pair he had slain were missed.

This time it was the second key, and again it was a white man, in so sorry a state it was a wonder he was alive.

"God," Bannon exclaimed yet again. "Webber, is that you?"

"It's me, blacksmith," the man said. He wore a crude eye patch and his left arm was permanently bent at an unnatural angle.

"They said you left your claim and went back east," Bannon told him. "What, two months ago?"

"They lied."

"Are you with us too?" Fargo asked.

"Damn right I am," Webber said.

The rest of the cells contained Chinese. They were in the same pitiable shape, and didn't speak English. But when Fargo said the word "Han" and pantomimed slitting his own throat, they understood.

Putting a finger to his lips, Fargo started up the stairs. Just below the ground floor, he stopped. Slowly raising his head, he counted seven Tong loitering near the main entrance.

Fargo swore. They couldn't go out that way. In the weakened state the prisoners were in, they couldn't have put up much of a fight.

Motioning to the others, he slipped up and around and down a narrow hall that would take them to the rear of the Pagoda.

That early, the building was quiet, and not many people were about.

They passed several chambers and nooks. At the next, the doorway glowed with lamplight.

Fargo signaled for the others to stop and risked a peek. It was a kitchen. Cooks were busily preparing the morning meal for the Tong and their master.

Quickly, Fargo went on by. No outcry was raised. He could only hope the others were as careful.

The corridor ended at a door that wasn't locked and didn't have a bolt. It opened to reveal the rising sun.

Fargo held it for the others and shut it behind them.

Arnold and Webber and the Chinese gazed about them as if they'd never seen the world before. Webber, in particular, was so overcome with joy, a tear trickled from his remaining eye.

"Where to?" Arnold asked. "I'll follow your lead. You've done right fine so far."

"Bannon's place," Fargo said.

"Why there?" the blacksmith asked. "That's the first place the Tong will look."

"I left my horse there," Fargo said. And his Henry was in the saddle scabbard.

"After that?" Webber wanted to know.

"We stay alive."

They hugged the backs of the buildings. Only once were they seen, by an old woman who came out of a shack with a basin of dirty water and upended it. She regarded them with no more interest than if they were squirrels, and went back in.

Fargo was in luck. The stallion was where he'd left it. While the men filed into the shop, he wedged the hatchet he'd taken under his gun belt, shucked the Henry, and jacked the lever to feed a cartridge into the chamber.

The main street was still largely deserted. An older Chinese pushed a cart. A woman was getting an early start on her wash.

Inside, the former prisoners were tearing like a pack of starved wolves into bread and biscuits and whatever else the blacksmith had handy.

"We don't have much time to spare," Fargo reminded them.

Arnold grunted. "Give us a couple of minutes. I'm so weak from not having enough to eat, I'm downright puny."

Webber nodded in concurrence, his cheeks bulging.

"Do you have a plan?" Bannon asked.

No, Fargo didn't. He was making it up as he went along. "We head off into the woods and lie low the rest of the day."

"Why not go after Han now?" Webber demanded between chews.

"You just said you're in no shape for it," Fargo replied. "We'll hit them after dark. It will give us an edge." Not much of one but he would take what he could get.

"I suppose that's best," Arnold conceded. "All I want is to get my hands on that runt."

In a few minutes they were ready. They took what food they could carry, along with a few other things.

Fargo rode, the rest walked. They made it to the end of the canyon undetected. Even after the forest closed around them he didn't feel safe until they had gone more than half a mile.

"I don't believe it," Arnold happily exclaimed. "We're out of there!"

"I thought I was a goner for sure," Webber said.

They and the Chinese were so exhausted, they lay right down and went to sleep.

Fargo heated coffee. He needed it for what he had in mind. Bannon stayed up, too, sitting across the fire, his big hands on his knees.

"So far, so good," the blacksmith said.

"Don't jinx it."

Bannon stared at the sleepers. "We don't stand much of a chance with this bunch, do we?"

"It's better than just the two of us."

"How come you're not resting?" Bannon asked, and answered his own question. "As if I can't guess. You're going after her, aren't you?"

Fargo nodded.

"Is that smart? What if you don't make it back? What do the rest of us do?"

"Light a shuck for Salt Lake City or anywhere else."

"In the shape they're in, how far would we get without your help?"

"I'm going," Fargo said, "and that's final."

By now the sun was well up and the wilds were alive with the warbles and chirps of birds. Somewhere, a raven cawed. A jay screeched from a trectop.

Fargo filled his tin cup to the brim a second time.

Staring into the flames, Bannon remarked, "Terry O'Brien might have a pistol you can borrow, if that would help."

Fargo hadn't thought of that. "It will." He intended to check on the O'Briens anyway.

"In fact," Bannon continued, "you might ask if he's got other guns he can spare. Our little army can sure as hell use them."

It wasn't much past eight by Fargo's reckoning when he climbed back on the Ovaro.

Bannon didn't hide his worry. "I wish there was some other way. If we lose you, we don't stand a prayer."

"If I don't make it back," Fargo said, "get hold of a federal marshal."

"It will take a company of soldiers to root those damnable Tong out."

Fargo raised the reins.

"By now they must know we escaped," the blacksmith tried a last time. "Likely as not, they'll be waiting for you."

"I'm still going."

"Damn, you're stubborn," Bannon said, but he smiled as he said it.

Hunan was in the full bustle of its daily routine. Fargo skirted to the south and followed the canyon wall until he came to the same stand of trees he had hid in with the women the day before. He tied the Ovaro where it wouldn't be seen and continued on foot.

The House of Pleasure was quiet at that hour. Few people paid for lovemaking so early in the day.

Fargo crept to the front but didn't show himself.

Four Tong were standing guard. Across the way, eight more were lounging in front of the Pagoda. Han wasn't taking any chances.

Fargo was debating how best to go about rescuing Mai Wing when who should come out of the Pagoda than the mistress of the House of Pleasure.

Madame Lotus exchanged pleasantries with the Tong. Whatever she said made them laugh. She turned and walked to the bridge, taking small steps, her hips swaying under her too-tight dress; she was a living, breathing, exquisite doll. She stopped in the middle, apparently to admire the sparkling water flowing underneath. Then, her hands folded in front of her, she crossed over.

Fargo smiled. Under his breath he said, "Never look a gift horse in the mouth." Raising the Henry, he centered the sights on her chest.

17

Madame Lotus smiled at an old woman and she smiled at two children and she smiled at a man carrying a rake and shovel. She smiled at the Tong in front of the House of Pleasure as she approached, and then Fargo took a step out of the shadows so she could see him—but the Tong couldn't—and her smile faded.

Keeping the Henry trained, Fargo pointed at her and crooked a finger.

Madame Lotus hesitated. She glanced at the hatchet men in front of her place. She was weighing whether she could reach them before he shot her, and made the right decision. She came over to the corner.

Fargo backed up and beckoned.

Frowning, Madame Lotus followed.

"Far enough," Fargo said. He had to get this over with quick before the Tong wondered why she had gone around the side of the building.

"We meet again," Madame Lotus said gaily, forcing a smile. "To what do I owe this unexpected honor?"

"Mai Wing," Fargo said.

"The stubborn one. The child who does not know when she is well off. What about her?"

"Have the Tong bring her out."

"She's not in my place," Madame Lotus said. "I don't know where—"

Fargo took a quick step and gouged the muzzle against a thin eyebrow. "One more lie and I splatter your brains all over the ground."

"You would shoot a woman?" Madame Lotus asked with a smirk.

"Look in my eyes."

Madame Lotus looked. Her smirk died and she coughed and shifted her weight from one foot to the other. "You are no gentleman."

"And the Tong are?" Fargo snapped. He gestured. "Move back far enough for them to see you and order them to bring Mai Wing out."

"They will wonder why."

"Say you want to talk to her."

"They will think it strange. I can talk to her inside."

"Give them any excuse you want."

"It will not be enough."

"Explain," Fargo said.

Madame Lotus had regained some of her composure. Folding her small hands, she said, "You appear to misunderstand my position. Yes, I run the House of Pleasure. I do so for Master Han. So long as I do so efficiently, he permits me to retain my position."

"You're stalling," Fargo said.

"Please. Hear me out. My life is in your hands, after all." Fargo frowned. "What else?"

"I am Master Han's servant. I have no say over anything else. I certainly have no say over the Tong. I cannot tell them what to do. Only Master Han can do that."

"Then ask them to bring her out."

"And if they refuse?"

Fargo thumbed back the hammer. At the click, she stiffened. "One step at a time, lady."

Madame Lotus swallowed. She took a few steps back and turned toward the entrance.

Fargo moved so his rifle was inches from her head. She could see it but the Tong couldn't. "Ask them, damn it."

"As you wish," Madame Lotus said. She was genuinely frightened. Clearing her throat, she called out in Chinese. A Tong answered. Madame Lotus said more and the Tong responded.

"Well?" Fargo growled.

Out of the corner of her ruby mouth, Madame Lotus said, "I asked that they please bring Mai Wing out to me. I told them Master Han said the girl could have some air. That if we show her we can be nice, she might be more receptive. A man has gone to bring her."

"Good lie," Fargo said.

"You have put me in a terrible position," Madame Lotus said. "Master Han is already upset with me because you took her and the sisters away."

That reminded Fargo. "Where are the Pous?"

"After half an hour with Master Han, they changed their minds and start work as pleasure maidens as soon as they heal."

"Pleasure maidens," Fargo said, and snorted.

"There is a subtlety to life that eludes you, I think," Madame Lotus said.

"I know a bastard when I meet one," Fargo said. "And a bitch."

Suddenly Madame Lotus tensed and squeezed her hands so tight, her knuckles were white.

"What?" Fargo whispered.

"Another Tong has just come out and is coming over to me. His name is Zhin. He is in charge of those who guard the House of Pleasure."

Fargo heard footsteps, and a man addressed her. It sounded to him as if Zhin asked a question, and she responded. For all he knew, she was telling Zhin about him. He couldn't take the chance. He stepped out behind her with the Henry pointed at the back of her head.

Zhin started to reach for a hatchet at his waist, and froze. He hissed in Chinese at Madame Lotus.

"What did he say?" Fargo asked.

"Master Han has given orders to all the Tong that you are to be killed on sight."

"Has he, now?"

Zhin hissed more Chinese, and Madame Lotus wrung her hands. "He says that I am to tell you they are doing as

you want and bringing the girl out. But really I am to drop flat when he tells me to and he will attack you."

"Not much for brains," Fargo said.

"He reminded me it is my duty to die for my master if need be."

"Why are you telling me all this?"

"To be honest," Madame Lotus said, "I very much want to live."

"Ask him if he wants to be shot."

"Excuse me?"

"You heard me," Fargo said. "Ask the son of a bitch if he wants to take a slug."

Madame Lotus spoke in Chinese. Zhin's answer was another sibilant hiss.

"He says he would be happy to die for Master Han."

"I never said anything about killing him," Fargo said. "Ask him if he would like to be shot in the balls."

Madame Lotus looked at him, her mouth agape.

"Do it, damn it."

Coughing, Madame Lotus quietly relayed the question. Zhin's eyes widened and he looked down at himself and gruffly replied.

"He wants to know why you ask such a thing."

"No brains at all," Fargo amended. "Say that if he so much as twitches, that's where I'll shoot him."

"You would shoot his manhood?"

"Clean off."

"Am I to deduce that you believe he values his private parts more than his duty to Master Han?"

"He's male."

"The distinction eludes me."

"If you had balls it wouldn't." Fargo wagged the Henry. "Tell him."

Madame Lotus complied. Zhin looked fit to breathe fire and spat a couple of words.

"He says that he hates you."

"I'll try not to lose sleep over it." Fargo shifted and fixed a bead on Zhin's crotch. "His men better fetch Mai

Wing out pronto or he can forget ever dipping his wick again."

Zhin's throat bobbed. Fargo had been right about him. Zhin growled something more to Madame Lotus.

"He says that he will do as you request. He asks that you not deprive him of his glorious staff."

"His what?"

"That is what he calls it."

Fargo almost laughed. He was keeping an eye on the Tong across the stream; so far none had noticed him. People passing by had but they minded their own business and walked on without raising an outcry.

Zhin growled again.

"What now?" Fargo said. "He doesn't want me to shoot his glorious walnuts either?"

"He says you are a fool to defy Master Han. He says you will never escape, that your doom is sealed."

"Tell him to give it a rest." Fargo gazed past Zhin at the Tong at the entrance. They were all looking at him, and his rifle. One started forward but stopped at a word from another.

"One thing I would like to know," Madame Lotus said, "is why you have put your life at risk for a girl you have only just met."

"She has a nice ass," Fargo said.

Madame Lotus gave him another incredulous look. "I begin to wonder if you are sane."

Fargo chafed at the delay. He couldn't hold the Tong at bay forever. His every instinct was to get out of there before he was in hatchet men up to his armpits.

"Tell me something," Madame Lotus said. "How far do you expect to get? The Tong have horses. They do not ride often but they can when they have to, and they will come after you."

"Let them." Fargo would pit the Ovaro against any horse in creation any day of the week.

"Should you succeed, where does that leave Mai Wing? She has no family in this country other than her grandfather. She has no American friends. She will be a stranger in a strange land."

"She'll do better than at the House of Pleasure."

"Will she, indeed?" Madam Lotus said indignantly. "For your information, my girls are paid well. Master Han lets them keep fifteen percent of all they earn."

"That much, huh?"

"If a girl applies herself it can be a large sum of money by Chinese standards."

Across the stream in front of the Pagoda, a Tong pointed in their direction.

"Where's my Colt?" Fargo asked.

"Your sidearm? I am sure I don't know."

"Ask Zhin," Fargo directed. "The Tong took it from me so he might know."

Madame Lotus translated.

The hatchet men over at the Pagoda were all staring and talking excitedly.

"Zhin says that it would have been turned over to Master Han to do with as he deems fit."

"Figures."

Moving in a body and unlimbering their hatchets as they came, the men at the Pagoda made for the bridge. In less than a minute they would be on this side.

"Damn it to hell," Fargo said.

"What is wrong? Are you mad about your Colt?"

"Get ready to duck."

"Whatever for?"

"A lot of coyotes are about to die."

18

The Henry held fifteen rounds. Sixteen, if Fargo had a cartridge in the chamber when he reloaded the tube magazine.

There was a saying to the effect that you could load a Henry on Sunday and shoot it all week. It lacked the power and range of a heavy-caliber Sharps, but when it came to spraying lead, it was the best rifle out there.

As the Tong from the Pagoda reached the near side of the stream and brought their hatchets out, Fargo commenced to do just that. He shot the first four, working the lever as fast as he could work it. At each blast a man in black tumbled.

The hailstorm broke the rest. They stopped in consternation, then sought cover.

Zhin stayed frozen but the Tong in front of the House of Pleasure didn't.

Fargo spun and shot the first one who came at him, shifted, shot the second. A third man raised his hatchet and screeched in fury and Fargo shot him smack between the eyes.

The pair who were left should have sought cover, too, but they didn't. He shot them dead.

Madame Lotus blurted an exclamation in Chinese, her hand to her throat.

Zhin bubbled with rage, and for an instant Fargo thought he would come at him.

On both sides of the stream, people were running and shouting and a few women were screaming.

"Hell in a basket," Fargo growled. Tong would come from all over now.

Stepping past Madame Lotus, Fargo slammed the Henry's

stock against Zhin's temple. Zhin sank to his knees, and Fargo slammed it again. Stepping over the sprawled form, he raced into the House of Pleasure.

As luck would have it, the Tong who had gone after Mai Wing was just returning with her. They'd stopped at the blasts of gunfire, and on seeing Fargo burst in, the Tong yelled and flourished his hatchet and attacked.

Fargo couldn't help thinking that anyone who brought a hatchet to a gunfight was a jackass. He shot the man through the head, ran to Mai Wing, and grasped her arm. "Can you run?"

"Yes," she said brightly, her eyes glistening. And then, "You came for me. Again."

"Later," Fargo said, and hauled her out into the sunlight.

Madame Lotus hadn't moved. Only now she held a slender silver dagger. "I will not permit you to take her."

"Get the hell out of the way," Fargo snapped. He could see Tong off up the street, in both directions.

"I must show my master I am loyal to him," Madame Lotus said. "If I kill you, he will be pleased. If you kill me, he will be pleased."

"You're loco, lady," Fargo said, and smashed the Henry's barrel against her chin. He might have broken her jaw or a few teeth but she had it coming for being a party to forcing girls into the life of a pleasure maiden.

"Oh my," Mai Wing said as the exquisite China doll crumpled.

Fargo grabbed her hand and ran. They made it to the stand of trees, and shoving the Henry into the scabbard, he swung aloft and lowered his arm for her to grab. Once she was behind him with her arms wrapped around his waist, he quickly reloaded the Henry and resorted to his spurs.

Hunan was in an uproar.

Fargo galloped west. His intent was to rejoin Bannon and the others. Checking on the O'Briens would have to wait.

A pair of burly Tong appeared at the end of a side street and moved to cut him off. Shouting defiance in Chinese, they threw themselves at the Ovaro, their hatchets gleaming in the sunlight.

"Goddamn idiots," Fargo growled. He shot both, the two cracks almost one sound, and shoved the Henry into the saddle scabbard to free his hands for riding.

Soon they reached the end of the canyon, and Fargo looked back.

Three Tong were after them on horseback.

"Son of a bitch."

"Sorry?" Mai Wing said into his ear.

"Hold on tight." Fargo reined to the north. He wouldn't risk leading the Tong anywhere near Bannon and the others. He would shake them off first.

It was a hard ride, but his confidence in the Ovaro was boundless.

For the next hour Fargo used every trick he knew. The Tong were surprisingly persistent. He was over five miles from the camp, deep in the mountains, when he finally lost them.

By then the Ovaro was lathered and in need of rest.

The next clearing Fargo came to, he drew rein. "We'll stop here for a while," he announced.

Alighting, Fargo held up his hands and Mai Wing slipped into them. As he lowered her, she pressed her body against his.

"Thank you for saving me," she said, "a second time."

"What are friends for?" Fargo joked. He let go of her waist but she didn't move. She was so close, her warm breath fanned his neck. "How are you holding up?"

"I am fine."

Fargo knew better. She must be hurting like hell from all her bruises. "Have a seat," he suggested. He chose a grassy spot and sank down, and a moment later she sank down next to him. Fact was, she almost sat on top of him. He moved a little to give her room and she moved so her side was against his. He wondered what she was up to and then saw the look on her face.

"Oh, hell."

"Sorry?" Mai Wing said sweetly.

"You can't be thinking what I think you're thinking," Fargo said.

Mai Wing smiled and kissed him on the cheek. "I am very grateful."

"There were no strings attached," Fargo informed her. "You might want to get some rest."

"I do not need any," Mai Wing said. "They put me in a room and left me, and I have been sleeping ever since. When that Tong arrived, I thought they were going to take me down and torture me more."

"We couldn't let that happen," Fargo said with a grin.

"You couldn't," Mai Wing said. "You put your life in danger once more to rescue me." She paused, then stressed, "I am very grateful."

"This isn't the time or place," Fargo said.

"Why not?" Mai Wing kissed him on the mouth. Not a quick peck but a soft, tender kiss that lingered. When she drew back, she asked, "Did you like that?"

"It was nice," Fargo said. He figured that would be the end of it. In her condition she was in no shape for the other.

Mai Wing looked him in the eyes and put her hands on his shoulders and kissed him with more passion. The tip of her tongue rimmed his lips. This time when she broke the kiss, she asked, "That one was better, was it not?"

"I forgot you were female," Fargo said.

"I do not understand."

"I wouldn't know where to touch you," Fargo tried to explain, "not without hurting you."

"Here is fine," Mai Wing said, and taking his hands, she placed them on her breasts.

"Watermelons, by God," Fargo said.

"I beg your pardon?"

Why not? Fargo reflected. They were safe enough and it would be half an hour before the Ovaro recovered. And her antics were stirring him down low. It had been a while, and if there was anything on God's green earth he liked more than making love to a woman, he had yet to make its acquaintance.

"Why do you just sit there? Don't you find me attractive?"

"Hell," Fargo said, and squeezed her tits.

Mai Wing groaned and kissed him.

Fargo sucked on her tongue and pinched her nipples through her shirt and she moaned deep in her throat. He didn't touch her body. Not with her wounds. But he recollected that her legs were untouched, and dipped a hand between her thighs.

Mai Wing pressed close. "You have wonderful fingers," she whispered in his ear.

Fargo caressed higher and she melted into him, kissing his cheeks, his eyebrows, his nose, of all things. His hunger grew. He smothered an urge to press her flat on the ground. It might hurt her.

They sat kissing and caressing for a long while. Then Mai Wing pulled back, smiled, and stood. Fargo figured that was that, but, no, she set to removing her clothes. She didn't take them all off; she bared her legs as high as her hips.

She had a small silken thatch. When Fargo cupped it, she sank onto his legs. He had to raise her up again to undo his belt and his pants and slide them down around his knees. He wanted to push them lower but Mai Wing couldn't wait.

To his considerable astonishment, she gripped his iron-hard pole, straddled him, and impaled her womanhood as neatly as you please.

Mai Wing gasped and arched her back. She said something in Chinese and switched to English. "It is like the morning dew."

Whatever the hell that meant. Fargo grunted. He had a lump in his throat and a keg of black powder about to go off between his legs.

"I have never made love to a man like you before," Mai Wing said.

"An American?" Fargo guessed.

"A man with a beard."

Fargo put his hands on her hips. Her sheath was moist velvet and gripped his member like a glove.

"Do I feel nice to you?"

"You talk too damn much," Fargo groused.

"I do more than talk," Mai Wing said, and gripping his arms, she commenced to pump her hips. Slowly at first, with

languid ease, teasing him, tempting him, arousing him, and then faster as she stimulated his need.

Fargo had to hand it to her. She knew just what to do. He was fit to explode.

Mai Wing abruptly stopped and locked her eyes on his. "One thing," she said with the utmost seriousness.

Here it comes, Fargo thought. She was going to say how fond she was of him, and did he have any interest in being with her from then until forever.

"I do not love you."

"What?"

"I do not do this because you have claimed my heart," Mai Wing said. "I do not do this because I want to be your wife. I think of you as a friend. Nothing more. Does that hurt your feelings?"

"Not a whole lot," Fargo admitted.

"Good. I do this to thank you for saving me, and for one other reason."

"I'd be curious to hear what it is."

"You will think I am silly. Or immodest."

"Try me," Fargo said.

"I am not sure you can understand."

"Damn it, woman."

Mai Wing smiled and kissed him on the mouth and looked down at where their bodies were joined. "I had an itch."

19

For a woman who had seemed painfully shy, when it came to lovemaking Mai Wing was anything but.

Fargo let her ride him to her heart's content, and ride him she did. For long minutes she rose up and down, her eyes slits, occasionally gasping or sighing or uttering a soft moan. Now and then she kissed him or nipped his ear or bit his neck.

All Fargo had to do was lean back and enjoy. Usually he ran his hands and his mouth over every square inch of a woman's body but her wounds kept his hands off most of her.

The feel of her wet sheath, the warm sun on his face and back—he could feel the tension drain out of him.

He'd been a bundle of raw nerves the past few days, what with so many people out to make worm food of him.

Mai Wing huskily said something in her native language as she dug her nails in deep.

"What was that?" Fargo asked.

"I said," she replied, and swallowed, "you are so big, and so hard, you excite me greatly."

"You're not half bad yourself."

Unexpectedly, Mai Wing stopped pumping. "Hold on. Half bad? Does that mean I am only half good?"

"No," Fargo said, chuckling. "You're plenty good. If you were a pleasure maiden, you'd have men lined up around the block."

"A pleasure maiden," Mai Wing said in disgust. "A woman should have the right to say who will and won't touch her. Is that not so?"

"I'm glad you gave me the right," Fargo said to flatter her.

Mai Wing tilted her head. "Something tells me, handsome one, that women do that a lot."

"There's been a few."

"Am I one of the best?"

Fargo thought back to some of the wild and lusty ladies he'd frolicked with. "You're up there," he tactfully replied.

Mai Wing smiled. "Good." She closed her eyes and pumped. "I want you to remember me as I will remember you."

Fargo let her do as she pleased. He wasn't in any hurry. He figured to return to Bannon and the rest after dark and then to go see about the O'Briens. And sunset was hours off yet. Plenty of time for him to enjoy himself.

He'd never had any woman ride him as long as Mai Wing. Most liked to get it over sooner. Not her. She pumped and squeezed and pumped and squeezed but somehow never quite brought him to the brink, as if she had perfect control over her pussy. It was remarkable.

Finally, though, Mai Wing cried out and moved faster and harder. She held on to his shoulders, her mouth wide, making sounds that a blacksmith's bellows would make.

Fargo grasped her hips and concentrated on not sliding out of her.

"Yes," Mai Wing said. "Yes, yes, yes. I am almost there."

Fargo pinched a nipple.

"Ahhhh!" Mai Wing exclaimed. She threw back her head and gushed with a violence her small frame belied, slamming against him as if she were trying to break him in half.

All Fargo could do was hold on for dear life and ride out the tidal wave. When at long last she subsided and collapsed, he brushed a bang from her eyes.

"Thank you," Mai Wing breathed.

"We're not done yet."

"Excuse me?"

"My turn," Fargo said. Firming his hold, he rammed up into her.

The whites of Mai Wing's eyes showed and she groaned

loud enough for them to hear her in Hunan. "You have a magnificent pecker. Is that the right word?"

"It'll do," Fargo said, "and my pecker thanks you."

She laughed.

Fargo let himself go. He thrust harder, faster, his pleasure mounting with each stroke, the friction and the wetness stoking his inner fire hotter and hotter until the keg of black powder detonated.

Afterward, it was his turn to collapse onto his back and smile. "Not half bad at all."

With him still inside of her, Mai Wing eased her breasts onto his chest and rested her cheek on his shoulder. "You are the best I have ever made love to."

"Had a lot of men, have you?"

"Only two, counting you."

Fargo looked down at her.

"There was a boy in China," Mai Wing said. "I was in love. I thought that one day I would be his wife. But my father disapproved and would not allow it. And then my father and mother and grandfather decided to come to your country." A tear trickled. "I will never see that boy again." She sniffled. "Or my parents."

"You might want to get some sleep."

"I wish they had never caught sick on the crossing. I wish they were still alive. I miss them so much. Now that my grandfather has betrayed me and sold me to Master Han, I am all alone in the world."

"Why did the old goat do that?"

"It is common. All the girls in the House of Pleasure were sold to Master Han as I was."

"Why do the other Chinese stand for it?"

"The Tong," Mai Wing said.

"There aren't that many of them. If all of your people rose up and fought, they could drive Han out or bury the bastard."

Mai Wing let out a sad little sigh. "It is not in our nature. We are taught from an early age to always obey. Our parents. Our teachers. Anyone in authority. And the Tong have the authority."

"You stood up to him," Fargo reminded her.

"My father always said I was a rebellious child. I guess he was right." Mai Wing closed her eyes. "Now if you will permit me, I am tired. Is it all right if I sleep a while?"

"Snore away," Fargo said. He could have used a nap himself. Stretching his legs out, he drifted into a pleasant dream where every painted doll in the House of Pleasure took a turn riding him.

The raucous cry of a jay snapped him awake. He'd slept longer than he liked; the sun was well on its downward arc.

Mai Wing was still sound asleep, her lips fluttering with every breath.

Fargo shifted to relieve a cramp and she opened her eyes. "Rise and shine."

"What time is it?" Mai Wing asked as she sleepily sat up and yawned.

"About four." Fargo eased from under her and began to put himself together.

"I thank you again for sharing your body. You are a good lover." Mai Wing set to dressing. "You dare not go back into Hunan. You know that, don't you?"

"I have to do it," Fargo said.

"If Han should get his hands on you—" Mai Wing didn't finish. She didn't need to.

It was a long ride to the clearing.

Mai Wing was in a gabby mood. He learned all there was to know about her childhood and life in China.

"We were very poor," she said at one point, "as were many in our province. There was little work, and the jobs that were to be had paid very little."

"From what I hear," Fargo mentioned, "the Chinese over here don't make all that much money either."

"Ah. But a little here is a lot back there when the dollars are converted into our currency. It is why when my father heard about the opportunities America offered, he couldn't wait to come. It is why some villages send nearly every young man to this country to work and send money home. But the men cannot bring their wives or their families, so it is very sad."

"They have to come whether they want to or not?"

"It is considered a great honor. No young man would refuse."

"More of that kowtowing," Fargo said.

"Sorry?"

"I could never be Chinese."

"Why not?"

"All that bowing and scraping wouldn't sit right," Fargo said.

"I think you have the wrong idea," Mai Wing said. "My people bow to authority but they are not slaves."

"Could have fooled me."

Mai Wing fell quiet after that. Fargo sensed that he had hurt her feelings but he was only speaking his mind.

The sun was a golden plate on the rim of creation when they neared the clearing.

Fargo rose in the stirrups but didn't see anyone moving about. He cupped his mouth to hail them, and a premonition came over him, a feeling in his gut something wasn't right. He shucked the Henry.

"What is it?" Mai Wing asked.

"Don't know yet," Fargo answered. "Hush."

The morning's fire had long since burned down. Several figures were sprawled near it, and at first Fargo took them to be sleeping. Only when he emerged from the trees did he see the red splotches. He quickly drew rein.

"Damn."

"Are they dead?" Mai Wing asked in horror.

"If they're not," Fargo said, "they're wasting a lot of blood." Dismounting, he held on to the reins.

Arnold, Webber, and the Chinese men from the dungeon were all dead. By the looks of things, they had been beaten to death. Arnold's face consisted of pulped flesh and broken bone. Webber's throat was crushed.

"The Tong's handiwork," Mai Wing said.

"You sure?" Fargo didn't see a single chop mark.

Mai Wing nodded and imitated striking her left hand with her right as if she were holding a hammer. "They used the flat side."

Fargo didn't see Tom Bannon anywhere. He did find drag marks, and the hoofprints of three horses. "The Tong who were after us," he deduced, "found them instead. Must have taken them by surprise. The poor bastards."

"This is partly our fault?"

"Bannon and the others should have been on their guard."

Fargo set about gathering firewood. When Mai Wing saw what he was doing, she lent a hand. Soon flames crackled.

As he was putting on coffee, Mai Wing folded her arms around her bent legs and asked, "What will you do?"

"Nothing's changed."

"There is just you now."

"It's never just me," Fargo said, and patted the Henry.

"I advise you to forget about Han. Let's you and me leave this place. Later you can come back with the marshal you have talked about."

Fargo grinned. "I've never been good at taking advice."

"What can you do alone except die?"

Fargo shrugged. "We all do, sooner or later."

20

Hunan was a beehive. Lights lit the streets and buildings. The opium den and the House of Pleasure were the most popular places in the camp.

From under a spruce at the west end of the canyon, Skye Fargo sat in his saddle, on the lookout for Tong. "I wish you'd listened to me, damn it."

"You swear a lot," Mai Wing said. "Do you know that?"

"Never noticed." Fargo had tried to talk her into staying at the clearing but she refused. He sensed she was a bit spooked by the deep woods. She was also worried the Tong might come back. He'd balked at bringing her but he couldn't leave her there if she didn't want to stay. So here they were, about to bait the lion's den together.

The north side of the canyon didn't have as many cabins and shacks and tents. Fewer people meant it was safer for Fargo to wind along the side streets and cross the small tracts of woodland still standing until he came to the O'Brien place.

Once again he drew rein.

Several of the windows glowed. A shadow flitted across one.

"They are home," Mai Wing whispered.

"So it seems." Fargo wasn't taking anything for granted where the Tong were concerned. "You stay here. And when I say stay here, I goddamn mean it."

"There you go again."

Fargo swung his leg up and over. He yanked the Henry from the scabbard, fed a cartridge into the chamber, and handed it to her. "Just in case."

Mai Wing held it as if it were about to bite her. "I have never shot a gun before."

Fargo demonstrated how to cock the hammer and instructed her in how to work the lever. She was still nervous. "I shouldn't be gone long," he said to set her at ease.

"Please don't be. I feel safer when I am with you. You inspire confidence because you have so much of your own."

"If you say so." Fargo was scanning the house and the yard.

"I have never met a man with so much force of will," Mai Wing declared.

"If you say so," Fargo repeated himself. He wasn't exactly sure what she meant.

"The force of life is strong in you."

"You can stop now," Fargo said. Palming the toothpick, he crept to the porch. He put his ear to the front door and thought he heard female voices. Checking the street, he rapped lightly. No one came. He rapped again, louder.

Suddenly the door opened and he was flooded in a rectangle of light. "Boyo!" Terrence O'Brien exclaimed.

"Keep your voice down," Fargo cautioned. He wouldn't put it past Han to have Tong watching their place.

"What is it?" Terry asked in concern.

Quickly, briefly, Fargo gave him the highlights. "Can I put my horse around back and bring Mai Wing in?"

"Need you ask?" the Irishman rejoined. "Our home is your home."

Fargo wasted no time. Only when the Ovaro was tied where no one could see it and Mai Wing stood in the O'Brien kitchen did he relax a little.

"You poor dear," Noirin said, touching Mai Wing's cheek. "My husband gave us some idea of what you've been through."

"They tortured you?" Flanna said, aghast. "How beastly can they be?"

"They are Tong," Mai Wing said in her simple way. "They do anything they please to anyone they want."

"They're devils, by God," Terry said. "And to think, I've stayed as long as I have."

117

"Are you hungry?" Noirin asked.

Fargo admitted he could stand a bite to eat.

Mai Wing said, "This one would be most humbly grateful to fill her belly."

"Don't you talk cute, gal," O'Brien said, and laughed his hearty laugh.

Fargo and Mai Wing sat at the table while Noirin and Flanna whisked about.

"It's a shame about Tom Bannon," Terry said. "I shudder to think what they might be doing to him." His face clouded. "And to think they had Arnold and Webber in that dungeon of theirs all this while. They deserve to die, every last one of the bastards."

"Your language, Terrence," Noirin scolded from over by the stove. "There are ladies present, in case it has slipped your mind."

"I'm sorry, woman. But damn it all, this has my dander up." Terry leaned on the table. "What are your plans, boyo?"

"To leave Mai Wing with you and go after the blacksmith."

Terry nodded. "I'm going with you."

Noirin stopped breaking eggs and turned. "You'd go off and leave us by ourselves?"

"Fargo, here, needs my help," Terry said. "He can't go up against those diabolical Tong alone."

"I suppose." Noirin glanced at Fargo and gnawed on her lower lip.

"You're staying here," Fargo said to Terry.

"Why? I have a shotgun and plenty of buckshot."

"There's less chance of being spotted if there's only one of us," Fargo said, which wasn't entirely true.

"I want to go and I'm going and that's final," Terry gruffly asserted.

"No," Fargo said. "You're not."

"No one tells me what to do, by God."

"I just did."

Terry puffed out his cheeks and glowered but it was mostly bluff. "Damn it, boyo," he said, and deflated. "It's not right."

"The women come first," Fargo said. "Or do you want your wife and daughter to go through what they did to Mai Wing?"

Terry glanced at her, and blanched. "If Han and his Tong so much as touch a hair on their heads, I'll blow them all to kingdom come."

"With a shotgun?" Fargo said, and grinned.

"No. With the black powder I have stored."

Fargo sat up. "The hell you say."

"Mr. Fargo, please," Noirin said.

"He does that a lot," Mai Wing threw in.

"How much black powder are we talking about?" Fargo wanted to know.

"Two kegs of the stuff. I bought it early on in case any of the prospectors had blasting to do. But no one wanted to buy any."

"Well, now," Fargo said.

A pot of coffee had been on the stove, keeping warm, and Flanna brought him a cup. She also set down cream and a bowl of sugar. "Word is all over camp about the Tong you killed."

"That it is," Terry said. "It was all anyone who came into the store talked about."

"Tell him about Lo Ping," Noirin said.

"He stopped by to ask if we had seen you," Terry related. "Him and those Hu brothers. I told him we hadn't seen hide nor hair of you and he must have believed me because he left without causing trouble."

"But we're under suspicion," Noirin said. "Now more than ever."

"The Tong haven't liked us from the beginning, dearest," Terry said. "What's your point?"

"That we can't afford to stay another day. As soon as Skye gets back, we should pack and go."

"As if Han will let us leave before he's good and ready to let us."

Once again Fargo nipped their dispute by saying, "First things first. You let me deal with the Tong. Then you can make up your minds whether to go or not."

"You're awful confident," Flanna said.

"That is exactly what I told him," Mai Wing said.

Fargo poured cream into his coffee and added a spoonful of sugar and gratefully sipped. A plan was forming but each step had to be carried out just right or he'd end up in an unmarked grave.

Noirin was preparing eggs and sausage. Flanna toasted bread and brought jam to the table.

Famished, Fargo ate as if the meal would be his last. Which, come to think of it, it might.

"What I'd like to know," Terry brought up, "is how the great and mighty Han expects to get away with his dirty deeds once the federal marshals hear about them."

"That's just it," Fargo said with his mouth full. "There won't be anyone left to turn him in."

"Exactly so," Mai Wing said. "My people will not do it, not only because they fear Han and the Tong. They do not trust your people."

"Why on earth not?" Niorin asked.

"A lot of whites do not like us because we are not white. I have seen a lot of hatred in the short time I have been in your country."

"The law is the law," Terry said. "It doesn't care what color a person is."

"My people do not know that."

"They need to learn it, then. They're Americans now."

"That is just it," Mai Wing said. "They aren't." She paused. "As much as I despise Han, I must admit he is shrewd. He has carved out a slice of China here in your wilderness. Once he has disposed of the last of the whites—"

"You mean us," Terry said.

"—he will rule Hunan as a mandarin of old. And there will be nothing your law can do to touch him."

"We'll see about that," O'Brien said.

"Two things," Fargo said. "Do you have a revolver I can use? And is your store locked?"

"I have a Colt upstairs you are welcome to use," Terry said. "As for my store, do you think I'd go off and leave it open for every scoundrel to help himself?"

"I'd like the key."

Terry's eyebrows met over his nose. "Have you ever used the stuff before?"

"A few times." Fargo spread jam on a slice of toast and bit off a piece.

"It has to be done just right. You don't want innocents hurt."

"What are you talking about, Father?" Flanna asked.

"A fitting end to Emperor Han," Terry replied, and laughed. "I'd pay money to see it."

"The important thing now," Fargo said, "is that you stay with the women and not let anything happen to them."

"Any of those bastard Tong try to come through my door, they'll do so without their heads."

"Honestly, Terrence," Noirin said.

"If a man can't swear on the eve of battle, when can he swear?"

"Battle?" Flanna said in amusement. "You make it sound as if we're going to war."

"We are," Fargo said.

21

There were more Tong guarding the Pagoda than ever. Not just out front but out back as well.

On his belly in a ditch forty yards from the rear of the tower, Fargo slipped his hand into his boot and drew the Arkansas toothpick.

Guards, yes, but no lanterns or lamps had been lit out back. It was a mistake that would cost them.

Fargo had fought Apaches. Lived with Apaches. Ate and made love and hunted with Apaches. And no one, anywhere, was stealthier. Apaches had no peers when it came to stalking and to hiding in plain sight. Some folks claimed they could turn invisible, which was ridiculous. They could do the next best thing—blend into any terrain so that they appeared to be part of it.

Fargo used their trick now. He crawled up out of the ditch and snaked from one patch of ink to the next. He moved incredibly slow. Slow was the key to not being spotted. He moved so slowly, it took half an hour to cover thirty feet.

The two Tong loafing on either side of the rear door were talking in low tones. Occasionally one or the other would laugh or chuckle.

Another half an hour, and Fargo was close enough to see that they were leaning on their shoulders facing each other, and had hatchets at their waists.

Fargo girded himself. He was set to spring when the door opened and out stepped Lo Ping.

The pair of Tong snapped straight as if they were soldiers on parade.

Lo Ping spoke to them and one answered. He gazed all about, made a short comment, and wheeled. The door shut after him.

Fargo wondered what that was all about. His best guess was that Lo Ping was making his rounds and checking with the guards to see that all was well.

But now the pair was more alert. One stretched and the other flexed his legs a few times.

Fargo either had to wait until they went back to leaning and talking, or do what he did. He was up in a blur and drove the toothpick's double-edged blade into the chest of the man who was stretching. He twisted, yanked it out, and was on the second Tong before the first realized he had been stabbed. The second man turned right into the toothpick. Fargo sank the sharp steel to the hilt in the man's throat and slashed outward.

It had been beautifully done. Neither managed to utter an outcry. They thrashed a bit, and the second man gurgled and bubbled fountains of blood.

The door was heavier than it looked. The smart thing for the Tong to do would have been to bolt it. He'd never be able to bust through without a battering ram. But they were overconfident and hadn't.

Chinese lanterns hung from pegs at intervals. The scent of incense hung heavy in the air, and muffled voices issued from the Pagoda's bowels.

Fargo drew the Colt. He wouldn't use it unless he had to. One shot, and every Tong in the place would be down on his head.

Finding the stairs to the dungeon wasn't difficult. Getting there was.

Twice Fargo heard someone coming. The first time he ducked into an alcove screened by hanging beads. He barely had time to steady the swaying strands when several Tong filed past. The second time he darted into a room that contained nothing but hatchets, row after row of them, hanging on the walls, enough to outfit an army.

He encountered no one on the stairs.

A single lantern cast feeble illumination over the dungeon. All the barred doors save one were open—it was the door to the cell he had occupied with the blacksmith.

Dreading what he would find, Fargo peered in. Someone was in there but he needed more light to see whom. Taking the lantern from the wall, he held it close to the bars.

Tom Bannon hung in shackles. He had been beaten about the head, neck, and shoulders to where he didn't resemble the man Fargo had left at the clearing earlier that day. Beaten so bad, he was close to death's door. His eyes were shut, his breathing labored.

"Bannon?" Fargo whispered. "Can you hear me?"

The blacksmith didn't reply.

While the door wasn't reinforced, if he tried to kick it in he'd probably break his leg before the wood gave way.

Fargo was about to turn and go in search of Lo Ping, who carried a large key ring, when he remembered that after he'd freed Arnold and Webber and the Chinese prisoners, he'd tossed the guard's keys into a corner. He wondered. Hurrying over, he moved the lantern back and forth. And there the key ring was, unnoticed in the shadows.

"Bannon?" Fargo said again when the door was open. He went over, wincing at the pulped flesh and broken teeth and bashed head. Certain the blacksmith was dead, he turned to go.

"Fargo?" the apparition croaked.

"I'm here."

One eye was swollen shut, the other barely visible. "The sons of bitches," Bannon said.

"I'll take you down and get you out of here." Fargo went to try the key in a shackle.

"Like hell," Bannon wheezed.

"I can't leave you like this."

"You know what you have to do."

"Hell," Fargo said.

"Do it."

"Bannon, I—" Fargo stopped. Words were useless.

"Do I have to beg? Is that it? If it was you hanging here I wouldn't like it but I'd do it for you. Do it for me."

"I'd have to use my knife."

"Do it, damn you." Bannon's voice broke and he begged in a whisper, "Please."

Fargo did as the man wanted. After, he wiped the blade on the blacksmith's shirt and stepped back and stared at the limp remains.

Sounds in the distance brought Fargo out of himself. Bending, he slid the toothpick into its sheath and pulled his pant leg down. Drawing the Colt, he made sure all six chambers were loaded. Then he stepped from the cell.

The sounds grew louder. More than one person was coming down the stairs.

Fargo shut the cell door as quietly as possible and melted into the shadows.

Light splashed the bottom of the stars. Two Tong materialized, one holding a lantern. They were talking and smiling. They went to the door and one peered in.

"American," he called out in bad English. "How are you?" He made a remark in Chinese to the other Tong and both laughed.

Fargo saw a hatchet on the hip of the man holding the lantern. Switching the Colt to his left hand, he glided up behind them. He didn't shoot. He yanked the hatchet free, whipped it high, and sheared it down into the crown of the Tong's head. It went in deeper than he expected. Wrenching it out, he shoved the Tong out of the way.

The other one spun. He saw his friend falling and the bloody hatchet in Fargo's hand, and pressed back against the cell door, bleating, "No!"

"Where's Han?"

"Where he always is," the Tong said.

Which Fargo took to mean on the throne in the audience chamber. He nodded at the cell. "Were you one of the ones who did that to him?"

"Me?" The man was breaking out in a sweat. "No. Others do it."

"You'd be piss-poor at poker," Fargo said, and arced the hatchet up and into the Tong's groin. The man screeched and clawed for his own hatchet but it was too little, too late.

Fargo cut him across the throat and stepped back to escape the spray.

It took a full minute for this last one to die.

Fargo holstered the Colt and helped himself to the other hatchet. With one in each hand, he climbed. He stopped below the first landing and peered over. Strangely enough, he didn't see Tong anywhere.

Fargo resumed climbing, faster now, taking two steps at a stride. There were no Tong at the second landing or the landings after that.

The doors to the audience chamber were closed.

Fargo put his ear to one but it was too thick to hear anything. Holding both hatchets in his left hand, he gripped the handle and pulled the door out a crack. From within came voices: Han's and Lo Ping's. To his surprise, they were speaking English.

"Has it been arranged?" Han was quietly asking.

"Your wish is always my command, great one," Lo Ping said in the same hushed manner.

"No one knows except you and me and the four men you have chosen?"

"No one," Lo Ping said.

"You are certain they can be trusted?"

"They are your most devoted servants," Lo Ping said. "Have no fear. The parents will be taken below, and the men I picked will take the daughter to your private quarters."

"Excellent," Han said. "Some might think me a hypocrite and I cannot have that."

"Never, great one," Lo Ping said.

They switched to Chinese.

Fargo had listened to enough. They must have been near the doors for him to hear them so clearly. Fate had given him a golden opportunity; he mustn't let it slip by.

He only hoped that most of the Tong were out searching for Mai Wing and him.

Taking a deep breath, Fargo hauled on the handle. The door swung wide, and there, not twenty feet off, walking away, were Han and Lo Ping, Han with his hands up his

sleeves, Lo Ping in the perpetual half bow he assumed when in his lord and master's presence.

Behind them, in silent ranks, were twenty or more Tong. Both turned.

Han recovered from his surprise first, and smiled his superior smile. "What a pleasant surprise. How delightful that you have paid me a visit."

"Master!" Lo Ping exclaimed.

Han ignored him. "Are you considering joining our benevolent society? Is that why you hold hatchets?"

Fargo had misjudged. He thought they were close enough to the doors that he could split their skulls and get the hell out of there before anyone could catch him.

"Cat have your tongue, as you Americans quaintly say?" Han taunted. "I don't know what madness has come over you, to attack me in my Pagoda. But I thank you for making this so easy." His smile widened. "As another of your expressions has it, you should make your peace with your Maker."

22

Skye Fargo was used to high odds. Sioux war parties, Apache war parties, outlaws, banditos, he often found himself pitted against more than one enemy at a time.

The Tong were poised to rush him, hands on their hatchets or hatchets in their hands. All they needed was a word or gesture from their master.

Fargo didn't wait for the word to be given. He whipped his right arm and threw the hatchet at Han. There were frontiersmen who excelled at throwing an ax or hatchet; he wasn't one of them. He seldom used an ax, save for chopping wood, and unlike backwoodsmen, he never carried a hatchet. So he wasn't surprised that he missed. Not by much, though. The hatchet flashed past Han's head, and for an instant stark fear animated those inscrutable features.

Almost in the same breath, Fargo threw the other hatchet at Lo Ping. It was only to delay the two and free his hands to use the Colt. But this time the hatchet streaked end over end and buried itself in Lo Ping's right shoulder.

Lo Ping screamed and clutched himself as blood spurted. Han roared in Chinese.

Fargo whirled and ran. He had come in the back way and he figured to go out that way, too.

Baying and howling like so many wolves, the Tong gave chase, sweeping toward the doors in a body.

Fargo was a fast runner. He had once entered a famous footrace, competing against some of the top runners in the country and a few from overseas. Now he fairly flew down the long hall.

Some of the Tong were fleet of foot, too, and grimly determined to avenge the insult to their lord. Two, in particular, were human antelopes. Legs pumping, they were gaining.

Fargo focused on running and only running. His worry was that their shouts would bring someone out of the side rooms directly into his path and slow him long enough for the main bunch to catch him.

The hall seemed to stretch for miles.

He had gone half its length when the patter of slapping sandals warned him the two fastest were practically nipping at his bootheels. He risked a look over his shoulder.

The swiftest Tong was almost close enough to throw his hatchet if he wanted to. The other one was a few yards behind.

Fargo wouldn't reach the rear door before they were on him. So he didn't try. Suddenly stopping and whirling, he shot the lead Tong in the head. The second one abruptly halted and made as if to throw his weapon. Fargo sent a slug between his eyes.

The rest of the black-clad pack howled in fury.

Fargo ran on. He had a good enough lead over the others that he was confident he'd reach the door ahead of them. In the dark of night he stood a good chance of slipping away.

He went another fifty or sixty feet and looked back to make sure none of the Tong were closing on him. They weren't.

He faced front—and swore.

An old woman holding a broom had stepped through a beaded curtain and was gaping at him in amazement.

Fargo started to shout, "Out of my way!" but he was already on top of her. They collided so hard, they both went down. She screamed, more in fear than pain. His left knee spiked with agony, and then he was up again.

Several Tong were dangerously near.

Fargo shot the first in the chest. The hatchet man pitched forward and the others avoided him by vaulting over the body.

Fargo shot the second as he landed, shot the third in midleap.

More bellows of fury filled the hall.

Fargo's knee hurt with every step but it didn't slow him any. He reached the back door and burst out, and tripped over the body of one of the guards he had knifed.

He stumbled, recovered, and was off into the night before the Tong spilled through the doorway.

Fargo made north toward the canyon wall. If they lit torches and tracked him, it would throw them off for a while.

When he at last turned to the west, he didn't head for the O'Briens' house; he made for their store. He slipped the key O'Brien had lent him into the back door and ducked inside.

Closing the door, Fargo leaned against it to catch his breath. Some light filtered in from the window of a nearby building. Not much, but enough that he could make things out.

He was annoyed at himself for not killing Han. It might come back to haunt him later.

Mopping sweat from his brow with his sleeve, he was about to straighten when he heard the stealthy scrape of a foot. Crouching, he cocked the Colt. He couldn't believe the Tong had gotten there ahead of him, but if they had, they'd find that cornering him and killing him were two different things.

"Skye? Is that you?"

"Damn," Fargo said, and rose.

A lithe form separated from the shadows. The scent of her perfume was stronger than usual.

"Flanna," Fargo said gruffly, "what in hell are you doing here?"

"Is that any way to greet me?" Flanna said, placing her hand on his chest and looking up into his eyes.

"Is your pa here?"

"No, just me." Flanna lightly kissed him on the chin. "I slipped out when they were talking to Mai Wing. Wasn't I clever?"

"You damned idiot."

"Here now," Flanna said, her feathers ruffled. "I have a

perfect excuse to tell them. I came to show you where to find the kegs of black powder."

"Your father already told me."

"I know." Flanna laughed. "But there are two kegs and you can't carry both so I'll say I came to lend you a hand."

"You shouldn't have," Fargo said, and pushed her back. "The Tong are after me."

"I'm not afraid of them."

"You should be." Fargo didn't have time to argue. He remembered the conversation he'd overheard between Han and Lo Ping. "Where's this hidey-hole of yours?"

"I'll show you."

The black powder was kept in their "cellar," as they called it, a square hole about four feet deep. To get at it, they had to lift some of the floorboards and set them aside.

"Wasn't this clever of my father?" Flanna said. "He didn't want the Tong getting their hands on it."

Fargo stiffened. From out in front of the store came the thud of pounding feet. Quickly, he covered Flanna's mouth with his hand and whispered in her ear, "Not a peep if you value your hide."

Whoever it was—and Fargo could guess who—they went on past.

He removed his hand. "From now on whisper. And don't make any noise if you can help it."

"Why would they look in here?" Flanna whispered. "They don't know my family and you are friends."

"Hell, girl," Fargo said. "You and me walked down the main street together the other day."

"Oh," Flanna said. "I forgot."

"Show me the damn kegs."

They were stacked one on top of the other in a corner of the hole. Fargo was surprised to also find guns and ammunition.

"Father hid them so the Tong couldn't get their hands on them," Flanna explained. "Turns out, they don't have much interest in firearms."

Fargo lowered his feet to the bottom. He was bending to

pick up the top keg when he heard more pounding of feet out in the street.

He couldn't say what made him do what he did next. Premonition, maybe, a gut feeling that the Tong would leave no stone uncovered.

Grabbing Flanna, Fargo pulled her down next to him.

"Hey!" she squawked.

"Quick," he said in her ear. "Help me cover the hole."

The boards weren't heavy but they had to be placed just so. As Fargo was sliding the second to last into place, a fist hammered on the front door and a voice called out in Chinese.

Fargo pushed Flanna low to the dirt, grabbed the last floorboard, and settled it over his head just as wood splintered at the front of the store.

"They're kicking in the door!"

Fargo clamped his hand on her mouth and held her tight as feet thumped on the floor above.

A lot of Tong were up there, going down every aisle. Voices rattled in Chinese.

Shouts outside apparently drew the Tong back out. The front door slammed and the store fell quiet.

Fargo eased his hand off Flanna's mouth but touched a finger to her lips so she would know not to say anything. It was nearly pitch-black. He became conscious of her warm body against his.

From the commotion in the street, the Tong were going from door to door.

Eventually Fargo felt safe in whispering, "It's all right. We can talk."

"My father will have a fit when he sees they broke the door in."

Fargo almost said they had a lot bigger worries than the damn door, but didn't.

"I reckon we're stuck here a while," Flanna said, not sounding the least bit upset about it.

"Until the coast is clear," Fargo said.

"Oh well," Flanna said, and snuggled closer. "We might as well make ourselves comfortable."

Fargo didn't see how. There was barely enough room for him to stretch out his legs.

Flanna shifted so her bosom was on his chest. "Nice, isn't it?"

"Behave."

"Whatever are you talking about? I'm not *that* kind of woman, thank you very much."

Fargo was glad shut-in places didn't bother him. He had a friend who couldn't stand to be hemmed in and wouldn't even enter a closet.

"Listen!" Flanna whispered. "Do you hear that?"

Fargo did. The creak of the front door. Some of the Tong must have been sneaking back in. Maybe they suspected something.

Feet shuffled to a stop overhead.

Fargo felt Flanna's fingernails dig into his arm.

Then one of the boards was lifted out and a hand gripped his shirt.

23

Fargo gripped the wrist above the hand and cocked his other fist.

"It's me!" Mai Wing whispered.

Flanna blurted, "What in the world?"

Fargo let go and removed more floorboards. Mai Wing helped. Standing, he pulled Flanna to her feet and boosted her out of the hole. Only then did he ask, "What are you doing here?"

"I came to tell you," Mai Wing said. "The Tong came to the house. They took Mr. and Mrs. O'Brien."

"What?" Flanna gasped in horror.

Fargo guessed what she would do and was out of the hole and had his arm around her waist as she took her second step toward the front door. "No, you don't."

"Let go!" Flanna struggled, pushing against him. "They're my parents, consarn you."

"Do you want to be thrown in the dungeon with them?" Fargo said, knowing full well that wasn't the fate Han had in store.

"Please," Flanna said. "I have to go help them."

"The only thing for us to do," Fargo said, "is to get them out of there. But we have to do it smart."

Flanna subsided, and trembled. "Why would the Tong take them? What have they done?"

"I heard some of what they said," Mai Wing said. "Your father heard them coming and your mother rushed me to the pantry and had me hide."

Flanna let out a soft sob. "I wish we'd left this terrible place weeks ago."

"Han thinks your parents have been helping Fargo," Mai Wing went on with her account, "so he wants to question them."

"If that's only all he does," Flanna said.

Fargo thought of how much Han delighted in torture, and held his tongue.

"I stayed hidden until the Tong were gone," Mai Wing related. "I knew Skye was to come here for the powder so I came to warn you."

"You did right fine," Fargo said. "Stay put, both of you." He crept to the front and peered out the window.

People were moving up and down the street but he didn't spot Tong. He returned to the women. "They've already searched here so it should be safe to stay a while."

"And my parents?" Flanna said.

"I'm going after them," Fargo said. "But first I rig a few surprises for Han and his boys." He gazed about the shelves. "I need empty bottles."

"I'll fetch them," Flanna offered.

"She is most upset," Mai Wing commented as the redhead hastened down an aisle. "I am sorry I brought sad tidings."

"O'Brien should have lit a shuck long ago," Fargo said.

"You wouldn't have, I bet, if this was your store."

"I don't have a family." Fargo dropped into the hole and lifted the first keg out, grunting from the exertion. He placed the second keg beside it.

"Is that enough for whatever you have in mind?"

"It's enough to blow this whole camp to hell and back again."

"You sound eager to do so."

"Han has it coming."

"Do you need a light to see by?"

"If I don't want to blow us to kingdom come," Fargo said. But a light would be seen out on the street. Either they covered the windows with blankets, which would arouse suspicion, or they did the next best thing: they hung blankets on the nearest shelves to form a sort of indoor tent.

"I have been meaning to ask you," Mai Wing said. "Whatever happened to Mr. Bannon?"

Fargo shook his head.

"Another life Han must answer for," Mai Wing said. "If he isn't stopped there will be no end to the killing." She brushed at her bangs. "There are days when I am ashamed that my people are such sheep."

"A lot of folks aren't fit to fight," Fargo said. "They don't have it in them."

"You are kind to make excuses. But I have learned that some things in life are worth fighting for, whether we live or we die."

"Do me a favor and keep an eye on Flanna while I'm gone," Fargo requested. "Don't let her come after me."

Just then the girl stepped out of the shadows. She had bottles in both hands. "What was that? I heard my name mentioned."

"I was wondering where you'd gotten to," Fargo lied. "Now I need a towel I can cut into strips. And lucifers if you have them."

Flanna hastened off again.

Fargo set to work. He placed the bottles in a row, then opened the first keg. He had to pour by feel and a lot of powder spilled over the bottles but he got it done. By then Flanna was back. He cut the towels into strips and plugged one end of each strip into a bottle.

"Oh, I get it," Flanna said. "You light the strips and they burn down and set the black powder off."

"That's the plan," Fargo said as he crammed another strip in.

"I would not have thought of this in a million years," Mai Wing said. "And my country invented black powder."

"I didn't know that," Flanna said.

"It is true. The world owes much of its culture to my people. We are not as backward as many in your country believe."

"Can't prove that by Han."

"He is Tong," Mai Wing said. "He is not typical of most Chinese."

"Ladies," Fargo interrupted. "We have to decide where you two will hide until I get back with Terry and Noirin."

The Tong had checked the store and been to the house but they might return.

"Hide, nothing," Flanna declared. "I'm going with you."

"Like hell you are."

"They're my parents. I have every right."

"You'd only get yourself killed, and me probably besides."

"I can be as sneaky as the next person," Flanna argued. "I'll bring a six-shooter and shoot any of the Tong who need shooting."

"Killed a lot of people, have you?" Fargo sarcastically asked.

"You know I haven't. But that doesn't mean I can't. The lives of my parents are at stake."

"My no is final," Fargo reiterated, wishing she would see sense. "Mai Wing, tell her," he said, thinking she would take his side.

"I would like to come as well," Mai Wing responded. "And I would very much like a gun if you will show me how to use it."

"Hell," Fargo said.

Flanna grinned. "Think of us as soldiers and you're our general."

"Hell, hell, hell."

"We'll take your orders. I promise."

"That's not the damn point. I can't watch you two and everything else at the same time. It's better if you hide out." Fargo had an inspiration. "And I know just where to do it." He pointed at the cellar. "Down there."

"It's too cramped," Flanna said.

"I would feel like—what do you call it?—a rat in a box?" Mai Wing said.

For two bits Fargo would bean both with a club and drop them in. "Ladies," he said as earnestly as he knew how, "tagging along is the worst notion either of you have ever had."

Damned if Flanna didn't cross her arms and stamp a foot and say, "You can't stop me."

"And if she goes, I go," Mai Wing said.

Fargo swore.

"My, oh my. That was colorful," Flanna said. "But you're

wasting time. Who knows what that monster is doing to my parents? Let's be on our way, or I will by God go without you."

"This one is ready to give her life if she must for her friends," Mai Wing proudly declared.

"I could shoot both of you," Fargo said. Instead, he hopped back down into the hole and rummaged through the guns and found a Smith & Wesson for Flanna and a Remington for Mai Wing. He loaded both and handed them up. "You'll need something to carry extra ammunition."

"I know just the thing," Flanna said, and whisked away. She was gone a couple of minutes and came back holding two pink tote bags with long straps. "Will these do?"

"They are very pretty ammunition holders," Mai Wing said.

"Any whiskey in this store?" Fargo asked.

"No," Flanna said. "It's not a saloon. Why would you even want whiskey at a time like this?"

"Beats the hell out of me."

"Has anyone ever told you that you swear a lot?"

Fargo sighed.

"When I was little if I used foul language my mother washed my mouth out with soap."

"Why are you telling me this?"

"I just think you could be nicer."

"I'm a lot nicer than Han."

"I've never heard him swear," Flanna said. "He's been to our store a few times and he always talked like a perfect gentleman."

Fargo began mentally counting to ten.

"Are you two ready?" Mai Wing asked. "We should start soon."

"I'm ready," Flanna said. "I want my parents safe and sound."

Fargo tried one last time. "There's nothing I can say or do that will change your minds?"

"Not mine," Flanna said.

"You have done so much for me," Mai Wing said. "I will do what I can for you."

Fargo balled his fists. He had half a mind to tie them up but they would likely fight him and where would that leave them?

"Well?" Flanna said. "Why are you just standing there?"

"Lead the way," Mai Wing said, smiling sweetly, "and we will follow."

"You have your very own little army," Flanna said.

"Yes," Mai Wing said. "Han has the Tong and you have us."

"God, I need a drink."

"There are times," Flanna said, "when I don't understand you."

"Yes," Mai Wing said. "Let us, as you Americans might say, go stomp Tong."

"God help us," Fargo said.

24

Fargo and his "little army" snuck out the back of the store and made their cautious way toward the Pagoda. Fargo made no more sound than the breeze. Flanna and Mai Wing did their best but their shoes scraped and their clothes rustled and once Flanna coughed and another time Mai Wing stumbled and almost fell.

Both women had their pink bags slung over their shoulders with the bag under an arm to steady the two bottles each carried. Their revolvers were tucked under belts taken from a store shelf and strapped tight around their waists.

Fargo was a bundle of raw nerves. The women didn't seem to realize that all it would take was the slightest of mistakes to see them in Han's clutches, or worse. Or maybe they did, and he should give them credit for more courage than most.

An unnatural quiet pervaded the camp. The Tong were out in force, searching and patrolling.

Once again the Pagoda loomed large.

From behind an outhouse Fargo studied the situation. A lantern had been lit and set near the back door. There were four guards now and one held a rifle.

"Pewwww," Flanna whispered. "Can't we hide somewhere else? I can't stand the stink."

"Hush up, damn it," Fargo said.

"We could go over by that cabin," Mai Wing whispered, indicating the one the outhouse was behind.

Fargo debated. To reach it they must cross forty feet of open space. "On your bellies," he said. "Hold the bottles in front of you and take it nice and easy."

Flanna dropped flat and crawled, whispering, "I'm part tomcat. Don't you worry about me."

Mai Wing eased down. "I like her," she whispered. "She has what you Americans call spunk."

"Too bad she doesn't have what we Americans call brains," Fargo muttered.

"Excuse me?"

"Crawl, damn it." Fargo followed, never once taking his eyes off the guards. They were alert, no doubt because they didn't care to share the fate of the ones he had stabbed.

The cabin was dark. Fargo took that to mean the occupants weren't home. He rose to his knees as the women had already done. "We made it."

"Did you think we wouldn't?" Flanna asked.

"We are good at sneaky," Mai Wing said.

Fargo promised himself, then and there, that when this was over, he was going to get drunk and stay drunk for a month.

"Skye?" Flanna prompted.

"Just thinking," Fargo said. "We can't go barging in with those guards there. We need a distraction."

"I could show myself to them and run off," Flanna suggested. "I bet they'd chase me."

"Not all of them," Mai Wing said.

"We have to lure the Tong from the Pagoda," Fargo clarified. "Not just those four."

"How in the world can we do that?" Flanna asked. "Set some of the buildings on fire?"

"Close," Fargo said. "Hand over one of your bottles."

"Be careful with it," Flanna said. "It's filled with black powder."

"Give me strength," Fargo said.

"They're not that heavy. See? I can hold it as easy as anything. You should know. You filled them."

"Flanna?"

"Yes?"

"Shut the hell up."

"Must you be so mean to her?" Mai Wing asked.

"You can shut the hell up, too."

"You are a strange man," Mai Wing said.

"Don't go anywhere," Fargo commanded. "No matter what you hear or see."

"What will we hear?" Flanna asked.

"Thunder," Fargo said. He crept to the front of the cabin. It was set back about twenty feet from the street.

People were passing by. Men, mostly. Few women and no children were abroad at that hour.

Across the stream at the House of Pleasure it was business as usual.

A pair of Tong had been posted at both ends of the bridge.

Fargo hadn't counted on that. He'd intended to slip across and place the bottle along the side of the House of Pleasure and light it. But he'd never reach the other side without being seen.

Hefting the bottle a few times, Fargo gauged the distance. He couldn't throw it far enough. It would fall short and kill passersby.

The creak and rattle of a wagon drew his gaze. A big wagon hauled by two plodding horses was coming up the street. The wagon was driven by an old Chinese; its bed was piled high with crates and covered with a canvas.

Inspiration struck. Fargo took a few steps, and froze.

Six Tong were out in front of the Pagoda. At the moment several were talking to a young woman and the others were listening.

Staying in the darkest patches, Fargo glided to the street.

The wagon's driver looked to be half-asleep. His chin was on his chest and his head bobbed with the rolling motion of the wheels.

Fargo fished the lucifers out of his pocket. He must time it just right.

At the Pagoda the young woman laughed. She was enjoying the attention.

The wagon rumbled abreast of Fargo. He waited until it was almost past, then darted over and around the rear to the other side. The driver didn't notice. Nor did the Tong at the bridge. Pacing the wagon, the bed between him and the

Pagoda, he struck the lucifer and lit the end of the makeshift fuse. The strip crackled into flame and the fire ate toward the bottle.

The wagon neared the bridge.

Fargo held the bottle close to his chest so the Tong wouldn't see the glow, and when the flame was barely a whisker's width from burning into the bottle, he threw it high, praying his aim was true.

Trailing a fiery tail like a miniature falling star, the bottle crashed down onto the roof of the House of Pleasure.

For a few moments nothing happened and Fargo feared the flame had been extinguished.

Then, with a tremendous blast, the black powder exploded. Sheets of flame erupted skyward and a huge cloud of smoke roiled and billowed. Parts of the roof rained down as fire spread across a jagged, gaping hole.

Literally everyone stopped and gaped.

The old driver jerked upright and hauled on the reins.

The Tong on the bridge and the Tong in front of the Pagoda ran toward the House of Pleasure. The people in front of it ran the other way. Within moments a panicked melee filled the street.

Fargo raced around the tail end of the wagon and over to the cabin.

The four Tong who had been at the back of the Pagoda came running to the front. They saw the flames and the smoke and sprinted toward the bridge to help their brother Tong.

From within the House of Pleasure rose screams and yells.

Fargo flew to where he had left the women. "Come on," he growled, hardly slowing.

"What did you do?" Flanna asked as she caught up.

"Spoiled a lot of lovemaking."

Fargo yanked the rear door of the Pagoda wide and sped along the narrow hall. He figured that Terrence and Noirin O'Brien had been taken to the dungeon and he was halfway to the stairs when Mai Wing surprised him by urgently calling his name.

Mai Wing had parted a curtain of beads. She nodded at something beyond. "Here," she said.

Fargo and Flanna ran back.

"I heard one of them try to call out to us," Mai Wing explained.

Trussed hand and foot and gagged, Terrence and Noirin O'Brien had been dumped on their sides in an alcove. Both struggled at their ropes and uttered muffled pleas for help.

"Mother! Father!" Flanna cried, and sprang to free them.

"Help her," Fargo said to Mai Wing as he took a bottle from her pink bag. Whirling, he ran to the front of the hallway. At the moment no Tong were in sight but he could hear feet pounding on the stairs that led down from Han's audience chamber.

Quickly, Fargo lit the cloth. This time he didn't wait. He stepped out and hurled the bottle at the stairs. The glass smashed with the same explosive results. Buffeted by a gust of hot air, Fargo ducked back as slivers of wood peppered the floor and the walls.

Both parents were free and Flanna was hugging her mother.

"You came for us," Terry said, rubbing his thick wrists.

"Did you think we wouldn't?" Fargo gestured. "Get them moving. I'll cover you."

"Boyo," Terry said, grasping his arm, "I can't tell you how grateful I am."

"Later," Fargo said.

The Irishman nodded and ushered the women toward the rear.

Smoke was pouring into the hall. A ruckus had broken out: angry shouts and cries of fear and what must have been oaths in Chinese.

The fire would spread rapidly; pine burned fast and hot.

Fargo backpedaled, watching for Tong, but none came after them. The hatchet men had their hands full with the fire in the stairs and the fire across the street.

Terry and the others were waiting. Fargo shut the door and led them to the west, saying, "Stay close and stay down."

Absolute bedlam reigned out in the street. Flames and smoke rose from both the Pagoda and the House of Pleasure.

"All that is your doing?" Terry marveled. "Remind me to never make you mad."

"It's Han I want," Fargo said grimly.

"And he wants you," Terry said, puffing as they ran. "You should have heard him. He practically flew into a rage at the mention of your name."

"Why didn't they put you in the dungeon?"

Terry chuckled again. "That's your doing, too. Lo Ping was going to take us there but Han said what good would it do since you'd escaped from it and returned for Bannon and killed more Tong and slipped away again. So they threw us in that cubbyhole."

"We were lucky to find you."

"I saw you and Flanna go past and tried to yell and that's when the Chinese girl heard me." Terry puffed as he ran. "Han will be madder than ever. He hates you, that one. I shudder to think what he would do if he got his hands on you."

"I'm going to give him his chance," Fargo said.

25

First, Fargo had to get the O'Briens and Mai Wing to safety. There wasn't room for all four of them in the hidey-hole in the general store. The Tong would go over every square foot of their house. The blacksmith shop, too, would be searched from top to bottom. So that left . . . "Grab enough food and blankets and whatever else you need to last a couple of days and I'll take you off into the woods."

"What if that damnable Han should get the better of you?" Terry bluntly asked.

"Head anywhere," was Fargo's advice.

The west end of the camp was largely deserted. Everyone had rushed to witness the conflagrations. Flames thirty to forty feet high licked at the night sky as they devoured the House of Pleasure and the Pagoda.

"I have to say," Terry remarked, "I don't like the idea of you doing my fighting for me."

"One of us should stay with the women," Fargo said, "and it's your wife and daughter."

They made a circuit of the house to be sure no Tong were lurking.

"In you go," Fargo said to the O'Briens. "And don't dawdle."

"In and out," Terry promised.

Mai Wing stayed with Fargo. Folding her hands, she gazed at the distant fires and said, "I have been most happy to know you."

"Hell in a basket, woman," Fargo growled. "You make it sound like I'm already dead."

"I was speaking from my heart. If you want to take me

with you when you leave, I would be honored to be your companion."

Fargo sighed.

"Am I to take that as a no?"

"It never fails," Fargo said. Poke a woman and she thought she owned you.

"I am not to your liking?"

"It has nothing to do with you," Fargo said. "I ride alone."

"One day, perhaps, you will change your mind."

Fargo was tempted to tell her it would be a cold day in hell but all he did was shrug.

Mai Wing smiled and reached over and touched his cheek. "You are a good man, Skye Fargo."

"No," Fargo said. "I'm not."

"I can prove it," Mai Wing said.

"How?"

"By logic. Han is a bad man, is he not? And you are the opposite of him, in your nature and your character. And what is the opposite of bad? It is good. Therefore you are a good man."

"What's taking them so long?" Fargo snapped.

Mai Wing chuckled. "Does my saying you are good make you uncomfortable?"

"No," Fargo said, "but all this blabber hurts my ears."

"Why do you pretend to be mean? I know the real you. We have shared our bodies. When two people do that, they share all that they are."

"All I shared was my cock."

"And a nice one it is. As nice as you are."

"Do you ever listen to yourself?" Fargo retorted.

Mai Wing laughed.

Fargo wasn't nearly as amused. He kept an eye on the street in case Tong came along but evidently they had all been pressed into service as a fire brigade and were combating the flames with buckets dipped in the stream. It was a losing proposition. Akin to spitting on a torch.

Given the size of the buildings and the rate the fire was spreading, the Pagoda and the House of Pleasure would be cinders by morning.

"Keep watch," Fargo instructed, and went around the back for the Ovaro. Climbing on, he rejoined Mai Wing and swung her up behind him.

"I like riding this way," she said, snuggling against his back and kissing his ear. "Does it excite you?"

Fargo wouldn't mind ripping off her clothes and doing her on the ground. But he answered, "Not a lick."

The O'Briens took too long but finally emerged laden with the things they thought they needed.

"What about horses?" Terry asked.

"We have the next best thing," Fargo said.

They went back up the street to the blacksmith's, and on to the rear and the buckboard.

Dismounting, Fargo said, "Help me throw everything off."

"But those are Tom Bannon's possessions," Noirin objected.

"If he comes back from the dead and wants them, they'll be right here."

"You have a tart tongue, Skye Fargo," Noirin said.

"Some ladies like it."

Noirin's eyes widened. "I sincerely hope you don't mean what I think you mean."

Even with all five of them, it took more than ten minutes. Some of the tools and bags were heavy, to say nothing of the anvil. Fargo and O'Brien handled that themselves.

Finally the buckboard bed was empty and the women made themselves comfortable. Terry climbed onto the seat.

Fargo swung onto the Ovaro and they were under way.

The flames were higher than ever, and the crackling and hissing as the timbers were consumed could be heard from one end of the canyon to the other.

"It's an inferno," Flanna said breathlessly. "I've never seen the like."

"They're the biggest fires I've ever seen, too," Noirin said.

"It is evil that burns," Mai Wing said in her simple way, "and evil always burns bright."

Terry shifted in the seat. "Amen to that, girl. It's too bad

if Han got out in time. It would be fitting if a fire sent him to hell."

"I wouldn't wish that on anyone," Noirin said. "Even my worst enemy."

"Which is exactly what he is," Terry said.

"Han's evil must be destroyed," Mai Wing said. "How is not important."

"There's a right and wrong way to do things," Noirin disagreed. "We shouldn't stoop to his level."

"Is there a right and a wrong way to kill a scorpion about to sting you?" Mai Wing countered. "Or a snake about to bite you?"

"He's not an animal," Noirin said. "He's a human being like the rest of us."

"He is not like us at all."

"The Book says that all men are sons and daughters of God," Noirin said. "Even a lowly heathen like Han. To treat him or anyone else as if they were animals is an insult to our Maker."

"Your Maker," Mai Wing said, "does not seem to care who lives or dies, or how they are slain."

"That's not true," Noirin heatedly replied. "We've escaped through his Grace."

"You are escaping," Mai Wing said, "because Fargo went to the Pagoda to rescue you."

Terry tried to intervene. "Ladies, ladies. That's enough, if you please. Argue some other time."

Noirin wouldn't let it drop. She turned toward Fargo. "How about you, Mr. Fargo? Where do you stand? Does Han deserve to die as a human being or as an animal?"

"I'm going to kill the son of a bitch any way I can," Fargo answered.

Terry laughed.

"I don't find it the least bit funny," Noirin complained. "The world would be a better place if more people respected the sanctity of life."

"Han sure as hell doesn't," Fargo said.

On that note they fell silent. They left the camp behind

and wound along for more than a mile. Fargo would have gone farther but Terry spied a clearing and wheeled the buckboard over.

"This will do us," he announced.

"Thank goodness," Noirin said. "I'm exhausted. I need rest."

Fargo dismounted and helped Flanna and then Mai Wing from the bed. Mai Wing pressed close, her body brushing his, and surreptitiously pecked him on the cheek.

"Do you think it's safe to start a fire?" Terry asked.

Fargo stared.

Terry coughed and said, "For the women's sake. My wife brought some tea. It would help quiet their nerves."

"Tong hatchets would quiet their nerves permanently."

"Point taken," Terry sheepishly responded. "No fire it is, then."

While the women spread blankets and prepared to bed down, Fargo took the two remaining bottles from a pink bag and slid them into his saddlebags. He checked that the Henry was loaded and that there were six pills in the Colt's wheel and went to Terry and offered his hand.

"What's this?"

"Just in case."

The Irishman gripped and shook. "Don't talk like that, boyo. I expect to see you again. You're a damn fine man. Anything you ever need, you have only to ask and it's yours."

"What will you do after Han and the Tong are taken care of? Leave or stay?"

"I haven't thought that far ahead," Terry admitted. "With him gone we wouldn't really have a reason to go, would we?"

Fargo stepped to the Ovaro and was about to climb on when a hand touched his shoulder.

"This one is most humbly grateful for all you have done in her behalf," Mai Wing said.

"You've already made that plain."

Mai Wing grew somber. "One thing. It is not enough that Han and Lo Ping are disposed of. To break the Tong, you must slay as many of them as you can."

"I figured on doing that anyway."

"Most especially slay the Hu brothers," Mai Wing said. "Should they live, they will take the place of their masters and nothing will have changed. They are just as cruel and heartless."

"Savvy that." Fargo gripped the saddle horn and forked leather, the saddle creaking under him.

"It has been an honor to know you." Mai Wing gave a slight bow and walked off.

Fargo reined around and looked one last time at the O'Briens.

On her knees on a blanket, Flanna smiled. "Please be careful. It would sadden me considerably if you were to die."

"Makes two of us."

Fargo had lingered long enough. He tapped his spurs and brought the Ovaro to a trot.

He had a war to wage.

26

The wind had died and a great cloud of smoke hung over the gold camp. In the first blush of impending dawn, the cloud was the color of blood.

An acrid odor filled the air and made Fargo want to sneeze. He made no attempt to hide; he rode down the center of the main street, his right hand on his Colt.

Smoldering black timbers were all that was left of the House of Pleasure. Scores of onlookers were watching the last timbers burn.

Across the stream the Pagoda had fared better; the ground floor had been spared. An exhausted fire brigade consisting of Tong and ordinary Chinese sat or lay in attitudes of fatigue.

Han stood on the bridge, his hands folded, gazing on the twin disasters with surprising calm.

Or maybe not so surprising, Fargo reflected. Han wouldn't want the other Chinese to see that he was no different from other mortals. Han got mad the same as they did; he had weaknesses the same as theirs.

Lo Ping was beside Han, looking as glum as a weasel could look.

The Hu brothers stood to either side, statues with hatchets at their waists.

When he was within earshot, Fargo drew rein. Alert for Tong with guns, he cupped his hand to his mouth and hollered, "Didn't that Pagoda have a roof?"

Everyone turned. Those sitting or lying down sat up or stood. Tong brandished hatchets and looked to their leader for the command to attack.

Han exhibited the same calm control. "You," he said with an icy stare. "I know this was your doing. Yet you dare return."

"I had to come back," Fargo shouted. "You have something I want."

"What would that be?"

"Your life."

Some of the Chinese understood English. Muttering and whispering broke out.

"You are not nearly as clever as you think you are," Han said, "and not intelligent at all to bait a spider in its own web."

Fargo made a show of glancing all around. "Spider? I don't see any spider." He looked directly at Han. "All I see is a polecat."

"Do you think you can insult me and ride away with impunity?"

"I'm not fixing to go anywhere until this is over."

Han smiled. "Are you so feebleminded that you do not realize there is only one way this can end?"

"Let's find out. I challenge you and your hatchet boys to a duel."

"You do what?"

"A duel. In the old days two men with pistols stood back-to-back and took ten paces and shot at each other. I'll just wait for you at the west end of the camp."

Han came to the near end of the bridge and leaned on the rail. "Do my ears deceive me? You have challenged me and my Tong to a fight?"

"You're too yellow to fight me alone."

Han drew himself up to his full height. "For that, American," he said, "you will die a most horrible death."

"Half an hour," Fargo said. "If you haven't shown up by then, I'll come looking for you." He cheerily waved at the people who were listening and wheeled the stallion.

One of the last structures on the street was a plank shack wide enough to hide the Ovaro behind. Taking the two bottles and the lucifers from his saddlebags, he tugged the Henry from the scabbard, crossed to the other side of the street, and sprinted around behind several tents.

Stopping at the last, Fargo hunkered. From his vantage he could see a long straight stretch of street. He set the Henry and the lucifers and bottles down.

He didn't doubt for a second that the Tong would come. He'd thrown down a gauntlet; Han must accept or be seen as weak.

A golden orb blazed the eastern horizon when figures in black loped into view. Two had rifles. Two others, revolvers. The rest, as usual, were relying on their hatchets.

Fargo lit the towel fuse to the first bottle.

Eight or nine Tong were passing the front of the tents when he stood and hurled the bottle. A Tong saw the flaming tail and yelled a warning—too late.

The bottle struck in the middle of the street and exploded. A fireball blossomed, and from within it issued horrid screams and wails.

A hatchet man's leg was blown clean off. Another lost an arm. A human torch shrieked and flailed at his burning black clothes and died shrieking.

Fargo braced for an attack but no one came running around the tents. They hadn't spotted him.

There was blubbering and a death rattle and a babble of voices in Chinese as the rest of the Tong rushed to the aid of the wounded.

Some were scanning both sides of the street.

Fargo lit the last bottle. He let the flames lick along the fuse until they were dangerously near the neck, and then he hurled it as he had the other.

This time several men in black shouted and pointed and many tried to scatter but they'd taken only a few steps when it went off.

The concussion shook the tent. Men were blown apart and screamed or burst into flame and screamed.

Charred body parts marked the center of the blast. A Tong gaped at the stump where his hand at been. Another, legless, flopped and blubbered.

The Henry to his shoulder, Fargo came around the tent.

He shot an unharmed Tong with a rifle, shot another who was holding a six-shooter as the man pointed it at him.

He shot a Tong with two hatchets, shot a Tong who charged him, shot a Tong who cocked an arm to throw.

And that was that. Those still able—a very few—broke and ran.

Fargo shot the Tong who was flopping and gibbering. He shot another with half a face. He shot a Tong bleeding from a dozen wounds.

No more needed to be put out of their misery.

Fargo reloaded. His best guess was that there couldn't have been more than seven or eight Tong left, including their lord and master and the weasel.

He strode up the middle of the street. The gold camp might as well be a cemetery. Not so much as a dog stirred. Everyone and everything, save for several horses at hitch rails, had fled.

The door to the general store was open and merchandise lay scattered on the floor. Sometime during the night it had been looted.

The blacksmith shop would never resound to the peal of hammer and anvil again.

Wisps of smoke rose from the Pagoda. A small portion of the second floor was untouched, and that was where a Tong with a rifle popped up and snapped off a shot that kicked dust next to Fargo's boot.

Fargo answered with the Henry.

Rising onto his toes, the Tong clutched his chest and pitched over the side. His rifle hit butt first. The Tong hit headfirst. A crunch, a splatter of blood, and his killing days were over.

Fargo approached the entrance. His back was to the bridge and it never occurred to him that a hatchet man might be hiding under it or beside it. The crunch of gravel warned him of his mistake. He spun but the Tong was already on him. A hatchet flashed in the sunlight. Instinctively, Fargo blocked with the Henry. Metal scraped on metal. The Tong hissed and swung at his thigh. Bounding back, Fargo sought to level the Henry but a jarring blow to the barrel knocked it from his grasp.

The Tong snarled and came at him swinging.

Fargo ducked, twisted, avoided a blow that would have practically cleaved his arm from his shoulder. He molded his hand to the Colt and fired as the Tong leaped at him, fired as the Tong was punched to the earth, fired as the Tong heaved up to come at him again.

Fargo faced the Pagoda and cocked the Colt. When no Tong rushed out, he quickly replaced the spent cartridges, twirled the Colt in his holster, and picked up the Henry. He also picked up the Tong's hatchet and tucked it under his gun belt.

Squaring his shoulders, Fargo entered the lion's den. No sooner did he cross the threshold than the Hu brothers were on him, one springing from the right, the other from the left. He whirled and got off a shot into one but the other smashed the rifle to the floor. He went for his Colt and triggered a shot and thought he scored but it had no effect. The flat of a hatchet caught him on the shoulder and spun him half around. He drove his boot into a knee. Fingers like metal speared from behind and wrapped around his wrist so he couldn't use his six-shooter. He drove his elbow back and was rewarded with a grunt.

Fargo dodged a hatchet that would have opened him from head to shoulders, shifted, and shot the Hu in front of him while at the same time he drew the hatchet from under his belt. He shot the Hu again even as he buried the hatchet in the arm that held his wrist.

One Hu was on his knees. The other was clutching his wrist in a vain bid to stem the spurt of scarlet.

Fargo shot them both in the face.

"Not so tough," he said to the bodies.

He cast the hatchet aside, holstered his Colt, and retrieved the Henry.

Warily moving to the long hallway, he parted the hangings.

Lo Ping was midway down, fleeing for his life.

Fixing a bead, Fargo waited. It wasn't a second later that the weasel glanced back and his face filled the Henry's sights.

Fargo stroked the trigger and Lo Ping tumbled and rolled to a stop.

Working the lever, Fargo advanced. He checked each room, each recess. He came to the alcove where they had found the O'Briens earlier, and there his quarry was, hands up his sleeves, and not as inscrutable as usual.

"Well," Han said.

"Hiding like the dog you are."

"A superior man does not do his killing. He has it done for him."

"Superior, my ass." Fargo pointed the Henry.

"I am rich."

"Good for you."

"I have money."

"I don't give a damn."

"I have jewels, emeralds and diamonds and rubies. They are yours if you spare me."

"Spare this," Fargo said, and squeezed. The walls amplified the blast. His ears ringing, he turned and walked out into the bright light of the new day.

The street was empty. No one tried to stop him. No one came out to thank him.

Once in the saddle, Fargo paused. To the west were the O'Briens and Mai Wing. He reined to the east.

The sun was warm on his back, and it was good to be alive.

LOOKING FORWARD!
The following is the opening
section of the next novel in the exciting
***Trailsman* series from Signet:**

TRAILSMAN #374
FORT DEATH

1861, in the heart of hostile country—someone is
killing scouts, and they have the Trailsman in
their gun sights.

The shot came out of nowhere.

One moment Skye Fargo was riding along a winding
track in the Salt River Range, and the next a lead hornet
buzzed his ear even as the boom of a rifle shattered the
morning air.

Fargo reacted instinctively. With a jab of his spurs, he
reined the Ovaro behind a slab of rock and dismounted.
Yanking his Henry rifle from the saddle scabbard, he
moved to where he could see the slope he thought the shot
came from.

A big man, broad of shoulder and narrow at the hips,
Fargo wore clothes typical of his profession: buckskins,
boots, and a high-crowned hat. A Colt that had seen a lot of
use was strapped around his waist, and a red bandanna in
need of washing was around his neck.

Fargo's lake blue eyes narrowed. He scanned the pines and spruce and firs without spotting the bushwhacker.

He'd heard reports the Bannocks were acting up of late, so it could be a hostile.

Or it could be an outlaw. He was far from any settlement, farther from any town or city, deep in the haunts of those who preyed on the unwary.

Either he waited the bastard out, or he went after him.

Fargo hunkered, the Henry across his legs. He had plenty of patience, and he wasn't due at Fort Carlson for another three days.

The post was named after the commanding officer.

It had been built specifically to keep the Bannocks and a few other tribes in check. Instead, it had stirred them up.

Time crawled.

Fargo refused to show himself until he was sure it was safe. And he wasn't thinking of just his hide. Anyone who knew prime horseflesh would have loved to get their hands on his stallion.

He took pride in the Ovaro. It was as fine a mount as any. If the shooter had brought it down, he wouldn't rest until the culprit was worm food.

Half an hour went by. Fargo was about convinced the culprit was gone when a shadow moved among the pines. Instantly, he snapped the Henry to his shoulder, fixed a bead, and fired.

There was no outcry. It could be he'd fired at a deer or some other animal but he doubted it.

Sinking onto his belly, Fargo crawled around the boulder and over to a log. Removing his hat, he raised his head high enough to see. Almost instantly a rifle cracked and slivers stung his cheek and brow.

Fargo ducked low. He touched his cheek and a drop of blood formed on his fingertip. He'd been lucky a second time; that shot damn near took out his eye.

Jamming his hat back on, Fargo crawled around the log

and into high brush. When he had snaked about ten yards he eased up into a crouch.

The woods were silent. The birds had stopped chirping and warbling, the squirrels had ceased their chatter.

Again Fargo wondered if it might be Bannocks. The latest word was that a band of young hotheads was killing every white they came across.

Above him, something moved. Someone was slinking down the slope in his direction, using every bit of cover to be had.

"Got you," Fargo said under his breath, and grimly smiled. Whoever ambushed him was about to learn that he wasn't the forgive-and-forget type. He was more an eye-for-an-eye hombre, and the devil be damned.

Fargo centered the Henry's sights on a two-legged shape but it promptly disappeared. Whoever it was, they were skilled at woodcraft.

Fargo did more waiting. All he wanted was a clear shot.

The sun climbed and no one appeared.

Fargo didn't like it. The shooter should be near enough by now for him to see or hear. He was about to rise and commence a hunt when he heard a sound that spiked him with rare fear: the Ovaro nickered.

Throwing caution to the wind, Fargo heaved erect and raced back. The shooter had circled and gone for his horse. Should the Bannocks get their hands on it, he'd likely never see it again.

He was so concerned for the Ovaro, he barreled around the rock slab with no thought to his own hide—and dug in his bootheels as a rifle muzzle blossomed practically in front of his face.

He had no time to level the Henry or draw his Colt.

He was as good as dead.

The rifle was a Sharps, and the man holding it had more whiskers than Moses. The man grinned and said, "Bang. You're dead."

For one of the few times in his life, Fargo was flabbergasted.

"What's the matter, pup?" the bearded man taunted. "Cat got your tongue?" At that he lowered the Sharps and let out a hearty laugh that more resembled the rumble of a bear.

"You son of a bitch," Fargo said, and hit him.

The punch rocked the other man onto his heels. Where most would have been mad and resorted to their hardware, the bearded bushwhacker only laughed harder. "You should have seen the look on your puss," he whooped, and roared anew with giant mirth.

A flood of emotions washed through Fargo: anger, resentment, relief, and finally amusement. Despite himself, he indulged in a good laugh of his own. "You're the craziest bastard I ever met, Tom. That stunt could have got you killed."

Bear River Tom, as he was known, was twice Fargo's age, with a craggy face and ruddy cheeks and a nose a moose would have envied. He wore buckskins, except the whangs on his were a foot and a half long and swished with every movement of his bulky body. "I got you, pup!" he crowed with glee. "I had you spooked. Admit it."

"You could have blown my head off, you jackass."

"If that was my intent, your brains would be leaking out of your noggin right this minute," Bear River Tom boasted. "You know how good a shot I am."

Yes, Fargo did, but that didn't excuse the practical joke. He reminded himself that Tom had always been the rowdiest scout on the frontier. "What if I'd shot you before I knew who it was?"

"That would have been plumb embarrassing."

Fargo shook his head, and sighed. "What are you doing in this neck of the woods, anyhow?"

"I got me an invite," Bear River Tom said. "From a pard of ours."

"You too?" Fargo said, thinking of the short letter he'd received from California Jim, a fellow member of the

scouting fraternity. He slipped his fingers into a pocket and touched it. "I got mine pretty near a month ago."

"Same here," Bear River Tom said. "Wonder why he wants to see us."

Fargo shrugged. He reckoned that California Jim had a good reason. They'd been friends a long spell.

"It'll be great to see him again," Bear River Tom said. Placing the stock of his Sharps on the ground, he leaned on the barrel. "So tell me, pup. Ever been to the Salt River Range before?"

"Been through it several times."

"Know it like the back of your hand, then?"

"Not that well," Fargo admitted. He'd always been on his way somewhere else. "What difference does it make?"

Bear River Tom shrugged. "Just asking. I don't know this country well, either." He gazed out over the array of peaks and verdant forest. "Fort Carlson wasn't built that long ago. The only scout I heard of working out of it is Badger."

"Emmett Badger?"

"Ain't he enough?" Bear River Tom said, and chuckled. "That coon has more bark on him than all these trees put together."

Fargo grunted in agreement. Emmett Badger had a reputation for being one of the toughest scouts alive. That took some doing, given that scouts were generally a hardy bunch who could hold their own with the Sioux and the Apaches.

"How about we fetch my cayuse and we'll ride on to the fort together?" Bear River Tom proposed.

Fargo grunted again. "Why not?" He wouldn't mind the company. Shoving the Henry into the saddle scabbard, he forked leather.

Bear River Tom was eyeing the Ovaro as if the stallion were a saloon filly. "That's a damn fine animal you've got there. You ever get in a mind to part with it, let me know."

"Part with?" Fargo said, and patted the Ovaro's neck. "Not while I'm breathing."

"Didn't think so. Word is that if it was a mare, you'd marry it."

"Go to hell."

Laughing, Bear River Tom cradled his Sharps and led the way up the mountain. As they passed through ranks of blue spruce he breathed deep and remarked, "God Almighty, I love the wilds. The mountains, the prairies, the deserts."

"Makes two of us," Fargo said.

"The only thing I love more than the wilds," Bear River Tom said, "are tits."

"Don't start," Fargo said.

"Yes, sir," Bear River Tom said. "I love a handful of tit more than just about anything."

"Here we go again," Fargo said.

"Fact is, when you think about it, tits should turn as many folks to religion as the Bible does."

"Were you in the outhouse when they were passing out brains?"

"Hear me out. Who else but the Almighty could have made it so tits are so much a part of our life from the cradle to the grave."

"I've lost your trail," Fargo told him.

"Think about it. We suck on tits for the milk when we're infants, we suck on tits when we're older to poke the females who have the infants who suck on the same tits for the milk, and we dream about tits in our old age to help pass the time. If that doesn't show planning, I don't know what does. God must like tits as much as we do." Bear River Tom grinned at his own brilliance. "You can see I'm right, can't you?"

"I need a drink," Fargo said.

Available now in hardcover
in the *USA Today* bestselling series

Tucker's Reckoning:
A Ralph Compton Novel

by
Matthew P. Mayo

In the two years since his wife and daughter died,
Samuel Tucker has wandered, drunk and increasingly
bereft of a reason to go on—until he sees two men
gun down a third and finds himself implicated in the
murder of the man he saw killed.

But Emma Farraday, the victim's niece, believes in his
innocence—and the two must reveal the machinations
of some wealthy and powerful men to prove it. If they
don't, Emma could lose the family ranch and Tucker
could lose his life—just when he's found a new
reason to live…

S0378

Frank Leslie

DEAD MAN'S TRAIL

When Yakima Henry is attacked by desperados, a mysterious gunman sends the thieves running. But when Yakima goes to thank his savior, he's found dead—with a large poke of gold amongst his gear.

THE BELLS OF EL DIABLO

A pair of Confederate soldiers go AWOL and head for Denver, where a tale of treasure in Mexico takes them on an adventure.

THE LAST RIDE OF JED STRANGE

Colter Farrow is forced to kill a soldier in self-defense, sending him to Mexico where he helps the wild Bethel Strange find her missing father. But there's an outlaw on their trail, and the next ones to go missing just might be them...

DEAD RIVER KILLER

Bad luck has driven Yakima Henry into the town of Dead River during a severe mountain winter—where Yakima must weather a killer who's hell-bent on making the town as dead as its name.

REVENGE AT HATCHET CREEK

Yakima Henry has been ambushed and badly injured. Luckily, Aubrey Coffin drags him to safety—but as he heals, lawless desperados circle closer to finish the job...

BULLET FOR A HALF-BREED

Yakima Henry won't tolerate incivility toward a lady, especially the former widow Beth Holgate. If her new husband won't stop giving her hell, Yakima may make her a widow all over again.

Available wherever books are sold or at
penguin.com

Charles G. West

"THE WEST AS IT REALLY WAS."
—RALPH COMPTON

Day of the Wolf

The mysterious mountain man called Wolf wants no part of the rampant war between the Crow and white settlers. But when three desperate women need his help in traveling across the Western plains, he finds himself in the thick of the conflict he's been avoiding all along

SIGNET
Published by New American Library, a division of
Penguin Group (USA) Inc., 375 Hudson Street,
New York, New York 10014, USA
Penguin Group (Canada), 90 Eglinton Avenue East, Suite 700, Toronto,
Ontario M4P 2Y3, Canada (a division of Pearson Penguin Canada Inc.)
Penguin Books Ltd., 80 Strand, London WC2R 0RL, England
Penguin Ireland, 25 St. Stephen's Green, Dublin 2,
Ireland (a division of Penguin Books Ltd.)
Penguin Group (Australia), 250 Camberwell Road, Camberwell, Victoria 3124,
Australia (a division of Pearson Australia Group Pty. Ltd.)
Penguin Books India Pvt. Ltd., 11 Community Centre, Panchsheel Park,
New Delhi - 110 017, India
Penguin Group (NZ), 67 Apollo Drive, Rosedale, Auckland 0632,
New Zealand (a division of Pearson New Zealand Ltd.)
Penguin Books (South Africa) (Pty.) Ltd., 24 Sturdee Avenue,
Rosebank, Johannesburg 2196, South Africa

Penguin Books Ltd., Registered Offices:
80 Strand, London WC2R 0RL, England

First published by Signet, an imprint of New American Library,
a division of Penguin Group (USA) Inc.

First Printing, November 2012
10 9 8 7 6 5 4 3 2 1

The first chapter of this book previously appeared in *Missouri Mastermind*, the
three hundred seventy-second volume in this series.

ALWAYS LEARNING   PEARSON

THE
TRAILSMAN
#373

UTAH
TERROR

by

Jon Sharpe

A SIGNET BOOK